Oliver Optic

In School and Out

Or, The conquest of Richard Grant. A story for young people.

Oliver Optic

In School and Out
Or, The conquest of Richard Grant. A story for young people.

ISBN/EAN: 9783744748605

Printed in Europe, USA, Canada, Australia, Japan

Cover: Foto ©Andreas Hilbeck / pixelio.de

More available books at **www.hansebooks.com**

IN SCHOOL AND OUT;

OR,

THE CONQUEST OF RICHARD GRANT.

A Story for Young People.

BY

OLIVER OPTIC,

AUTHOR OF "THE BOAT CLUB," "ALL ABOARD," "NOW OR NEVER,"
"TRY AGAIN," "POOR AND PROUD," "LITTLE BY LITTLE,"
"RICH AND HUMBLE," "THE RIVERDALE
STORY BOOKS," ETC.

BOSTON:
LEE AND SHEPARD, PUBLISHERS.
NEW YORK:
LEE, SHEPARD AND DILLINGHAM.
1873.

STEREOTYPED AT THE
BOSTON STEREOTYPE FOUNDRY,
19 Spring Lane.

TO

EDWARD JENKINS HOWE

This Book

IS AFFECTIONATELY DEDICATED

BY HIS UNCLE.

THE WOODVILLE STORIES.

IN SIX VOLUMES.

A LIBRARY FOR BOYS AND GIRLS

BY OLIVER OPTIC.

PREFACE.

THE second volume of the Woodville Stories contains the experience of Richard Grant, " in school and out." We are sorry to say that Richard had become a bad boy, and was in the habit of getting into the most abominable scrapes, some of which are detailed in the first chapters of this book. But he is not what is sometimes called a vicious boy, for he has many good qualities, which redeem him from absolute condemnation. There is something noble in his character, which is the germ of his ultimate salvation from the sins which so easily beset him.

Richard, like thousands of others, finds his strongest and most dangerous foe within his own heart; and the conquest he achieves is not a triumph of mind over matter, of force over force, but of principle over passion, of the good angels in the heart over the invading legion of evil ones.

Richard's experience is full of stirring incidents; and while the author hopes therein to realize the expectations of his partial young friends, he begs them to remember that these exciting events are only the canvas upon which he has endeavored to paint the great change wrought in the character of the hero. There is a moral in the story, and though the author has not attempted to "point" it, he hopes his young readers will feel it, even if they do not see it.

Again it affords me pleasure to acknowledge my indebtedness to my young friends for the kind reception given to my books. I trust that this, the twentieth volume of my "Stories for Young People," will not disappoint their hopes, or fail to improve their minds and hearts.

WILLIAM T. ADAMS.

DORCHESTER, Oct. 26, 1863.

CONTENTS.

8   CONTENTS.

IN SCHOOL AND OUT.

IN SCHOOL AND OUT;

OR,

THE CONQUEST OF RICHARD GRANT.

CHAPTER I.

"Now, steady as she is," said Sandy Brimble-com, who lay upon the half-deck of the Greyhound, endeavoring to peer through the darkness of a cloudy night, which had settled deep and dense upon the Hudson, and obscured every object on the shore. "Steady as she is, Dick, and we shall go in all right."

"Ay, ay; steady it is," replied Richard Grant, who was at the helm. -

(11)

"Port a little! Port a little!" added Sandy, a few moments after, as he discovered the entrance of a little inlet, which was the destination of the Greyhound.

"Shut up your head, Sandy!" replied Richard, in a low but energetic tone. "You might as well publish our plan in the newspaper as speak as loud as that."

"Port a little more," said the lookout forward.

"What's the use of hallooing port?" answered Richard, impatiently. "Don't you see the mainsail shakes now?"

"You will be on the rocks in half a minute more."

"Let her go about, then, and we will get a little farther to windward before we try to run in."

The Greyhound came over on the other tack, and stood away from the shore a considerable distance. The wind was very light, and the current was against them; so the progress of the boat was necessarily very slow.

"Now, Sandy Brimblecom," said Richard, when the boat had made a third of the distance to the opposite shore, "we might as well go back to Woodville, and go to bed, as to attempt to carry this thing through, if you are going to bellow and yell like a mad bull."

"I didn't think I spoke very loud," replied Sandy.

"Didn't think so!" sneered Richard. "Any one might have heard you clear across the river."

"O, no, Dick; not so bad as that."

"You spoke too loud, at any rate, and you might as well go up and tell 'Old Batterbones' what we are about as talk half so loud as you did."

"Come, Dick, you have said enough," replied Sandy, who did not relish all the reflections that were cast upon his conduct.

"You are as stupid as an owl; I thought you had some common sense."

"That'll do, Dick; I don't want any more of that kind of blarney; and if you don't shut up, you or I will get a black eye."

Richard did not seem to have much doubt which of them would obtain this ornamental tinting of the physiognomy, for he immediately changed his tone, and did not venture to apply any more unpleasant epithets to his companion. Sandy had obtained some reputation as a fighting character, and was virtually the champion of the ring among the boys in the vicinity of Whitestone.

" Now be more careful, this time, Sandy," said Richard, as he put the boat about upon the other tack.

" Don't give me any more lip, Dick, and I will do any thing you want," replied Sandy, mollified by the altered tones of his friend.

" Don't get mad; we have no time to quarrel, if we mean to put this thing through to-night."

" I am ready to put it through, but I have no notion of being treated like a slave or a fool," said Sandy, as he lay down upon the half-deck, and began to gaze into the gloom ahead of the boat. " Luff a little," he added, as he discovered the dim outline of the shore.

" Luff, it is."

This time, both boys spoke in a low tone, and the want of harmony which a few moments before had threatened to break up the enterprise, and end

in a game of rough and tumble, was removed.
The Greyhound, under the skilful management of
Richard,—for there was not a better sailor of his
years on the Hudson,—was thrown into the inlet
without touching the rocks which lay at the entrance.

Sandy, with the painter in his hand, jumped
ashore, and made fast to a small tree on the bank.
Neither of the boys spoke a loud word, and Richard carefully brailed up the sails, so that their
flapping should not attract the attention of any
person who might be in the vicinity.

" Now, Dick, if you will follow me, I will lead
you up to Old Batterbones' garden," whispered
Sandy, when the sail boat had been properly
secured.

" I will follow you. Have you got the bag ? "

" Yes — all right "

Richard followed his companion up the steep
bank of the river, across a field, till they came to
a fence, where they paused to reconnoitre.

" Now be careful, Sandy," whispered Richard,
nervously, " for I wouldn't be caught in this scrape
for the best hundred dollars that ever was."

" I don't want to be caught any more than you do," replied Sandy.

" Well, it won't make so much difference with you as it will with me."

" Won't it! Don't you think my neck is worth as much to me as yours is to you ? "

" I don't mean that, of course. Your father is a carpenter, and people won't think half so much of it if you are caught, as they would in my case."

" My father never was in the Tombs if he is a carpenter," growled Sandy.

" That's mean," said Richard. " You know he was put there for nothing at all."

" It isn't half so mean as what you said. If you think you are so much better than I am, what did you ask me to come with you for ? "

" I don't think I am any better than you are."

" Yes, you do; and you may go ahead with the game; I won't go any farther."

" Don't back out, Sandy. Have you got scared ?"

" I'm not scared; you are too big for your boots."

" No, no, Sandy, I didn't mean any thing of the sort."

" Didn't you say it wouldn't make as much difference with me as with you, if we got caught?"

" I only meant that people would talk more about me than they would about you."

" Perhaps they would, and perhaps they wouldn't. In my opinion, I'm as good as you are, any day."

" Of course you are; I never doubted it. Come, Sandy, we've run together too long to fall out now."

" I don't want to fall out, or back out; but I don't want to be snubbed, every ten minutes, about my father's being a carpenter."

" I won't say another word, Sandy. I didn't mean any thing."

" All right, my boy. I don't live in a big house, and my father isn't rich; but I'm just as good as any other fellow, for all that. If you didn't mean any thing, I'm satisfied."

" If I thought you were not as good as I am, of course I shouldn't go with you."

This conversation was carried on in a very low tone, while the boys were seated by the fence.

2 *

When Sandy's injured honor was healed, and the son of the rich broker of Woodville had acknowledged that the other was his equal, they were again ready to proceed with the business of the enterprise. Richard was not content with the homage which his companions could render without any sacrifice of self-respect, but he exacted the right not only to command them, but also to be indulged in the use of opprobrious epithets.

Sandy, as the " bully" of his circle, could not quietly submit to the domineering style of the rich man's son. He was willing, for the sake of sharing in the " loaves and fishes," which Richard had to distribute, to compromise far enough to be ordered in a gentlemanly way ; but he would not tolerate any invidious comparisons. Richard had a fine boat, and Sandy was very fond of sailing, which made him sacrifice some portion of his dignity as the champion of the ring. Richard was usually well supplied with money, which was a scarce article with the son of the journeyman carpenter, and boys bow down to the Mammon of this world, as well as men.

Richard patronized Sandy because his hard fist and abundant muscle rendered him a powerful and influential person. It was easier to buy the champion than it was to whip him, and the broker's son had conquered the bully by paying for the oysters at Bob Bleeker's saloon in Whitestone, and by permitting him to use the Greyhound when he wished. Richard had a great respect for muscle. If Sandy Brimblecom's father had chosen to pursue his peaceful avocation in any other locality than Whitestone, Richard Grant might have been the champion of the "P. R." The advent of Sandy had produced a fight, in which Richard, though he behaved to the satisfaction of all his friends and supporters, was severely punished. His friends called it a drawn battle; but Richard did not think it advisable to have the question definitely settled, and Sandy was acknowledged as the champion.

Richard respected the boy he could not whip, and they had become friends, or, at least, associates. It is scarcely necessary to inform the intelligent young readers of this book, that the moral standard of both boys was very low; for those who can fight simply to find out which is "the better man," have a very inadequate conception of what constitutes true dignity and nobility of character. "Muscle" and "backbone" — fighting ability and courage — in a good cause, are to be respected, and men and boys will always pay them due homage; but fighting for its own sake is mean, low-lived business — the most vicious of vices.

Sandy was satisfied with the explanation of his patron, and rising from his seat under the fence, he looked over into the garden, and listened for any sounds which might indicate an obstacle in the way of the enterprise; but not a sound could be heard except the chirping of the crickets and the piping of the frogs. With a great deal of care, he climbed to the top of the fence, and then listened again.

"Does he keep a dog?" whispered Richard.

"I don't know; I don't care, either," replied Sandy, as he dropped from the fence into the garden.

Richard climbed over with the same caution which

his companion had used, and after following him for some distance, reached a patch of watermelons, which appeared to be the destination of this night expedition.

"Get down on the ground!" whispered Sandy, who had already prostrated himself. "You will blow the whole thing if you stand up there."

"Open the bag, and let's fill it up. quick!" replied Richard, as he picked a large melon from the vines, and handed it to the other.

"What's. the use of picking such a melon in that?" snarled Sandy. "It isn't ripe. Can't you tell the ripe ones by the feeling?"

"No; I can't."

"Stick your thumb nail into them. Here, you take the bag, and I will pick them. We don't want to lug off melons that are good for nothing."

Richard took the bag, and placed the fruit in it as fast as Sandy gathered it. In a few moments the bag was full, and the young marauders commenced their retreat with all the haste which a proper caution would permit. The bag was large and . heavy, and it required their united strength to carry it

The garden proved to be something like an eel trap — it was easy enough to get into it, but very difficult to get out. Near the melon patch there was a piece of corn, by the side of which lay their path out of the enclosure. They had gone but a short distance when they heard a rustling in the corn behind them, and before they could make out the cause of the noise, a strong hand grasped the collar of each of them.

"We've caught you, my lads!" exclaimed one of the men, who had seized Richard.

It was an awful scrape: so thought the broker's son; and Sandy, notwithstanding the difference in their social standing, was of the same opinion.

CHAPTER II.

RICHARD JUMPS OUT OF THE FRYING-PAN INTO THE FIRE.

RICHARD GRANT was the son of a rich man, but he was neither any better nor any worse for this circumstance. He had been in a great many sad scrapes before the one in which the reader now finds him. It was not the first time he had taken that which did not belong to him.

In his father's garden there was an abundance of watermelons, and he had always been plentifully supplied with all the fruits in their season. He had, therefore, no excuse for stealing melons. There could be no excuse, under any circumstances, for stealing. He did not need them; he did not even want them.

But Richard was fond of exciting adventures, and it was simply the love of fun which had

prompted him to visit the garden of Mr. Batterman. I hope none of my young friends will think
this even palliated his offence. If he did not have
the motive which act1ates the common thief, he
was certainly more to blame than if he had
needed or wanted the product of his theft.
Stealing for fun cannot be any better than stealing from the love of gain, or to provide for one's
necessities.

Richard Grant is the hero of this volume; but I
shall not wink at any of his vices or inconsisten-
cies on this account. That he may not be utterly
despised, however, I may say of him that he had a
great many redeeming qualities. He was generous
to a fault, and his impulses were generally worthy
and noble. He was ready to give to the needy,
and to fight for the oppressed. He was kind-
hearted, and nothing but the love of sport could
induce him to violate the rights, or injure the feelings, of others. He lived upon excitement, and
was not always very choice of the means which he
used to procure it.

Richard's father had not been able to bestow

that care upon his moral education which his temperament required. He needed discipline, and the want of it was seen in his daily life. Mr. Grant was conscious of the boy's needs, and he frequently talked to him about his vicious course; but words did not supply the want; he required a more active treatment.

Sandy Brimblecom was as little disturbed by his conscience as his more wealthy companion. As long as he could stand upon an equality with an heir of Woodville, he was satisfied to let all moral questions take care of themselves. The two boys who sailed in the Greyhound on the eventful night of their introduction to the reader, were well mated in every respect. Either was ready to follow the lead of the other, without asking whether he was doing right or wrong. If there was any fun to be had out of the enterprise, both were ready to engage in it.

They had got into a bad scrape this time, for Mr. Batterman had the reputation of being a very hard man. He had suffered a great deal from the depredations of fruit thieves. He carried on a large

business in raising fruit and vegetables for the
New York market. It was not pastime to him,
but bread and butter — the means by which he
supported his family and accumulated his property.
Those who stole fruit from his gardens robbed him
of so much of his income; and he was not in the
humor to submit to these exactions.

In several instances he had taken these petty
marauders before the courts, and caused them to
be fined; but as this course did not remove the
evil, he had taken the law in his own hands, and
severely punished some of the juvenile offenders.
For this reason, among the boys he was called
"Old Batterbones," which was only a slight cor-
ruption of his real name.

Of course Richard and Sandy had no idea of
being caught when they embarked in this plunder-
ing expedition. They had taken extraordinary precautions to prevent such a catastrophe; but the
farmer was constantly on the watch, and they had
fallen into the trap which he had set not spe-
cially for them, but for any who might invade his
grounds with malicious intent.

RICHARD IN TROUBLE.   Page 27.

The person who held Richard by the collar, and whose finger nails had already left their marks upon his neck, was no less a person than " Old Batterbones" himself; and from the manner in which he shook his prisoner, he seemed determined to make good his title to the sobriquet the boys had given him. The person who held Sandy in his grasp was the farmer's foreman, who fully sympathized with his employer in his views of discipline.

Richard struggled, and Sandy struggled; but they might as well have attempted to escape from the grip of an iron vise. The farmer and his man held them fast; and the more their prisoners squirmed, the more they shook them, and the more they seemed to enjoy the satisfaction of shaking and choking them.

" We've caught you, my lads," said Mr. Batterman several times.

" Let go of me," growled Richard, his anger fully aroused by the rough treatment he was receiving.

" I'll let go, you young villain, when I've done with you, but not before. I'll teach you to steal

my melons; and then you can go home and tell
your father how it is done," replied the farmer,
as he twisted the cravat of the poor boy till he
could hardly breathe.

Sandy, finding that any violent resistance was
hopeless, submitted to his fate with the best grace
he could command; but he only waited his chance
for something to turn up that would afford him an
opportunity to escape. He intended to use his
wits, rather than his muscle, on this occasion; and
his prudence saved him from some portion of the
hard usage that was bestowed upon his companion
in misery.

"Keep cool, Dick," said he, in a low tone,
when he saw that his friend was wasting his
strength and adding to his discomfort by useless
resistance to the fiat of destiny.

Richard profited by this hint; and when he became calm and reasonable, the farmer relaxed his
grasp, and permitted him to breathe with more
freedom.

"Who are they, Bates?" asked the farmer of
his foreman.

"I don't know them; it is so dark I can't make them out," replied Bates.

"We'll take them up to the barn, and see what they look like."

"They have been here before, I think," added the foreman. "I am pretty sure I saw them the other night."

"No, you didn't," said Richard, testily. "I never was here before."

"Perhaps you never was, my boys; but when chaps like you go far enough to steal, you don't stand about a lie or two to cover it up. Now, boys, you may take up that bag, and carry it to the barn."

"I won't carry it," said Richard, promptly.

"Won't you?" And the farmer again applied the twisting process to his cravat, till the boy's strength was almost gone from the choking sensation.

"Let go of me! You'll choke me to death!" gasped Richard, who had never before been so roughly handled.

"Will you carry the bag up to the barn, then?"

demanded Mr. Batterman, as he eased off the pressure upon the prisoner's throat.

" No, I won't ! " replied Richard.

" Now, I think you will," said the farmer, as he resumed the torture.

" Come, Dick, we may as well do it. It is no use to kick ; we are in for it, and you had better make the best of it," interposed Sandy, who was disposed to get off as cheaply as he could.

" I won't touch the bag ! I'll die first ! " gasped Richard, whose rage had now reached the boiling point, and there was no more reason in him than in a mad dog.

" He's a hard one," suggested Bates.

" But he shall come to it, or I'll break every bone in his body," answered the farmer.

Richard, insane with passion, and choking with rage as well as from the discipline of Mr. Batterman, commenced a tremendous struggle for freedom and self-preservation. He sprang towards his captor in an ineffectual attempt to hit him, or to scratch out his eyes with his finger nails. Failing in his efforts in this direction, he began to use his nce s as vigorously as a three-year old colt, and succeeded in planting two or three hard kicks upon the shins of the farmer.

Mr. Batterman was a large and powerful man, and the efforts of Richard were as puny as those of a lamb in the fangs of the lion. He foamed and struggled till his strength was exhausted, and his conqueror permitted him to drop upon the ground.

" You've killed him," said Sandy, very much alarmed at the apparent fate of his friend.

" If I have, that's his business, not mine," answered the farmer, without betraying any remorse at what he had done.

But Richard was not killed, or even very badly injured. The choking had deprived him of all his strength; but a few minutes' respite from persecution restored him in a great measure, and he attempted to get up, when he was promptly seized by the farmer again.

" Will you carry the bag up to the barn, or will you try some more of the same sort?" asked Mr. Batterman, in a tone which fully indicated his intention to resume his harsh treatment.

32   IN SCHOOL AND OUT, OR

" I can't carry it," replied Richard, in an altered
tone, which was, at least, suggestive of a " caving
in" of his obdurate will.

" You carried it very well before you were caught,
and perhaps you can again," sneered the farmer.

" Come, Dick, take hold of the bag," said
Sandy. " It's no use."

" I wasn't brought up to do that kind of work,"
replied Richard, whose pride, quite as much as his
self-will, prompted him to refuse to do the degrading office.

" Take your choice, and be quick," said Mr.
Batterman, preparing to apply his disciplinary pow-
ers again. " Take hold of the bag at once, or
I'll shake the life out of you."

Richard could not stand another dose of the
farmer's exhausting medicine, and he sullenly seized
the bag, while Sandy took hold of the other side.
Bates and the farmer kept close to them, so that
there was no chance to break away. After chan-
ging hands several times, they reached the barn, and
placed the melons in the position designated by
their tormentors.

" Now, who are you?" asked the farmer, when they had disposed of the bag.

" None of your business." answered Richard, in a low, sullen tone.

" You haven't got enough of it yet. Bates, bring the lantern, and fetch a cowhide with you, while you are about it."

Richard did not like the sound of this last order. It was ominous of a painful and degrading opera-tion, a process of discipline to which he had never before been subjected. The idea of being whipped was almost as terrible as that of being shot through the head or heart.

" Will you tell me your name, young man?" demanded the farmer, when the foreman had gone. " Let me inform you in the beginning, that I am in no humor to be trifled with. You can answer me or not, just as you think best."

" I would rather not tell my name," replied Richard, in a subdued tone.

The son of the rich broker of Woodville had conscientious scruples on this point; for though he did not scruple to commit the theft, he was fully

alive to the disgrace of being exposed. The good
name, the worldly reputation of his family, seemed
to be of more value than a conscience void of
offence before Him who readeth all hearts. To
speak of the sin of the act was but to utter trite
and commonplace words, which could be found in
any cheap catechism; but to mention the disgrace
attending the exposure of that sin, was to touch
him where he was keenly sensitive.

"You must tell me your name," said Mr. Batterman, firmly. "What is your name?" he added,
turning to Sandy, whom he now held with one
hand.

"Sanderson Brimblecom," answered he, for he
had no family reputation to guard.

"Now, yours?" said he to Richard.

The broker's son made no reply. He had now
too much respect for Mr. Batterman to irritate him
with words, and too much respect for the name he
bore to connect it with the theft he had committed. He waited in silence till Bates came with
the lantern.

CHAPTER III.

RICHARD FINDS THAT NO CHASTENING SEEMETS TO BE JOYOUS.

"Tell him who you are, Dick," said Sand :, when Bates appeared with the lantern. " Wha's the use of trying to cover up your name, when the light will blow the whole thing?"

" Well, Dick," added the farmer, adopting the name Sandy had used, " if you don't tell me who you are, I shall see what virtue there is in that cowhide."

" My name is Richard Grant," replied the broker's son, sullenly, and with the feeling that he had sacrificed all his manhood by giving up the point.

" Ah, then you are the son of Mr. Grant, of Woodville !" sneered Mr. Batterman. " I don't wonder you didn't want to tell your name, for stealing melons isn't a very respectable business."

"I am willing to pay for the melons, and let the matter drop where it is," said Richard, who was so far humbled as to be willing to compromise with the owner of the stolen fruit.

"I am not exactly willing to let the matter drop where it is. You are the son of a rich and respectable man, and you ought to know better than to steal; and I am going to give you a lesson which I hope you will profit by."

"I will pay double price for all the melons, if you will let me go."

"I wouldn't let you go if you would pay ten times the value of the melons. I want to teach you better than to steal; and when I've done with you, I don't believe you will want to steal any more of my fruit."

"What are you going to do?" demanded Richard, very much disturbed by the decided tones of the farmer.

"I'm going to give you a sound thrashing."

"No, you are not," said Richard, who would rather have died on the spot than submit to the humiliation of a flogging.

"You will see whether I am or not. It's no kind of use for me to take a rich man's son like you before the court. Your father would pay your fine, and you would laugh in your sleeve, and call it a good joke."

"You have no right to flog me," protested Richard.

"Perhaps I haven't; but I'm going to do it, if I have to suffer myself for it. I am going to have the satisfaction of curing you of stealing my melons."

Bates had taken hold of Sandy again, and Mr. Batterman prepared to make good his promise. By the light of the lantern Richard saw the hard face of the farmer. It was stern and forbidding, and he felt that he meant all he had said. How could the son of the owner of Woodville submit to the disgrace of being whipped? At home he was treated with respect and consideration. The servants took off their hats to him. His father, in his sternest moments, had never hinted such a thing as corporal punishment.

It seemed absolutely impossible for him to sub-

4

mit to the farmer's terrible remedy, but there was
no way to avoid it. He had offered to compromise,
but nothing would satisfy his relentless captor.
The punishment was to be inflicted in the spirit
of revenge rather than from a sense of duty, which
made it all the more intolerable to think of. He
was not to be whipped for his own or the public
good, but to satisfy the malice and revenge of
" Old Batterbones."

He decided not to submit to the infliction ; but
he might as well have decided not to let the sun
rise on the following morning, or to stop the Hudson in its majestic flow to the sea. His own experience, so dearly bought in the garden, had shown
him that he was utterly incapable of any successful
resistance. He looked around him for the means
of escape, and racked his brain for some expedient
that would enable him to checkmate his unwieldy
opponent ; but he looked in vain, and thought in
vain. There was nothing upon which to hang even
the faintest hope of resistance or escape.

The farmer held him by the collar, and the terrible instrument of torture was raised over his head.

It fell, and Richard writhed with the pain, not of the body alone, for the blow seemed to penetrate to his soul. It lacerated his pride, his self-respect, more than it did his legs. He trembled like an aspen leaf, as much from intense emotion as from the smart of the stroke.

Richard was no coward, but he would have begged off, if he could have done so with any prospect of success; but he might as well have pleaded with the ocean to hold back its destructive waves, as with Mr. Batterman to stay his hand, before his revenge was satisfied. Another and another blow fell. The pain was so severe that the culprit could not endure it, and the quick-falling strokes soon kindled a fire in his soul which neither prudence nor policy could check. It burst out in a raging flame of passion, which caused him to roar like a mad-bull, and to kick, bite, and struggle like an imprisoned tiger.

All this resistance only added to the spite of his persecutor and he laid on the blows till his own strength failed him. In vain 'Sandy remonstrated with Richard upon the folly of his course,

and begged him to keep cool, as though a severe
flogging was one of the light afflictions of this
world, that may be endured with patience by a
philosophical temperament.

"Old Batterbones" had exhausted himself in the
struggle. His "wind" was gone; and he gave up
because he could do no more, rather than because
he was satisfied with the extent of the punishment.

"There, Mr. Richard Grant, of Woodville, when
you want to steal any more melons of mine, think
of that," said the farmer, as he cast the culprit
from him.

"You'll have to pay for this," groaned Richard,
who felt as though he had endured all the tortures
of the Inquisition.

"Perhaps I shall," puffed Mr. Batterman; "but
if you have got enough to make you a wiser and
a better boy, I shall be perfectly satisfied."

"I'll be revenged on you for this, if it costs
me my life, exclaimed Richard, whose soul smarted
even more than his body.

"Shut up, now!" said the farmer, angrily, "or
I'll give you some more."

Richard did shut up, for the incident had developed a grain of discretion in his composition, if
nothing better — though nothing better could be
expected from a flogging inflicted in the spirit of
malice.

" Now, my boy," said the farmer, turning to
Sandy, when he had in some measure recovered
his breath, " we will see what we can do for you.
You are not a fool like the other fellow, and your
wisdom will serve you a good turn."

Sandy made no remark in reply to this speech
of Mr. Batterman. He had made up his mind to
submit with all the philosophy he could bring to
his aid. He had been flogged before. It was not
a new institution to him, as it had been to his
companion in iniquity. He looked upon a flogging
as one of the necessary evils to which a fast boy
must submit; and though he did not think it was
all for the best, he was disposed to make the best
of it. The thrashing was the gate by which he
was to escape from a bad scrape.

The farmer bore less malice towards him than
towards his friend. He had offered no resistance,

4 *

and been measurably humble under the discipline
of misfortune. The blows were lighter and less in
number, and when a dozen strokes had been ad-
ministered, Mr. Batterman was satisfied, and so
expressed himself. At the same time he volun-
teered an opinion that Richard was the real sinner,
and had led the other into the mischief — a position which Sandy took no pains to controvert.

But Sandy, though he was a philosopher, and an
embryo man of the world, did not submit to his
punishment in silence. He was not a Stoic, and
every blow extorted from him a cry of pain, which
was as politic as it was necessary. He labored to
convince the farmer that he was suffering severely
from the castigation, so that he might be the
sooner satisfied with what had been done. Com-
pared with that which Richard had received, his
whipping was light. When it was finished, he
was surprised that he had got off with so little ;
and he congratulated himself upon the strategy
which had so sensibly diminished his portion.

"Now, boys, you can go. If you are satisfied,
I am; and when you want to steal any more of

my fruit, just remember my treatment of fruit thieves," said the farmer.

" You haven't seen the end of this yet," replied Richard, as he moved off, his skin and his proud spirit smarting in unison.

" You haven't seen the end of it either, if you don't keep a civil tongue in your head."

Richard was tempted to enter immediately upon the work of revenging himself for what he had suffered, and when the farmer spoke, he picked up a couple of stones, with the intention of throwing them at his tormentor; but Sandy, cool and self-possessed in the hour of tribulation, dissuaded him from this insane course.

" No use, Dick; drop the stones, and we will pay him off at another time, when we can do so without danger."

Richard listened to this prudent advice, and concluded to adopt it, though he was impatient to be revenged upon the farmer. He was not satisfied with Sandy. He had not been sustained in his resistance to the barbarous conduct of their captor. He thought his companion had been tame

and mean-spirited, he had submitted so quietly to
his punishment; and when they had got out of
the hearing of Mr. Batterman, he roundly reproached
him for his pusillanimous demeanor.

"I don't want to call you any hard names, Dick,
but in my humble opinion, you were a downright
fool," replied Sandy. "It's no sort of use to
pound a stone wall with your naked fist. You
don't hurt the wall any."

"I like to see a fellow show some spirit,"
growled Richard. "I thought you had some spunk;
but you caved in, and took your flogging as meekly
as though you had been one of the saints in Fox's
Book of Martyrs."

"I don't know any thing about your martyrs,
but I hadn't any notion of getting a double licking, as you did. You got four times as much as
I did, just because you were fool enough to resist.
If there had been any use in fighting, I would
have fought as big as you did."

"I like to see a fellow stand by another when
he gets into a scrape," whined Richard.

"Do you mean to say I didn't stand by you?

Did I run away from you ?" demanded Sandy, indignantly.

" You couldn't run away. The man held you
fast, or you would have done so."

" It's very easy for you to talk. I did all I
could to make you act like a reasonable fellow;
but you were bound to be a fool, and you got all
you bargained for."

Richard made no reply to his companion's taunts,
for his philosophy was beginning to commend itself
to his common sense, as he thought of the difference in the two floggings, and realized that it was
all owing to his own stupidity. They walked along
in silence, till they reached the Greyhound, but
still with " thoughts too big for utterance."

" A pretty condition I am in to go home," said
Richard, as he took his place at the helm.

" You will be all right in a day or too," replied
Sandy, consolingly.

" What will my father say ? "

" If you are fool enough to let him know about
it, I don't care wha he says."

"How can I help it? The blood is running down my legs now. My skin is all cut up."

"Wash off the blood, and don't let any body see your legs."

"I could kill Old Batterbones," added Richard, grating his teeth.

"We'll pay him off."

"I'll have my revenge, if I die for it."

"I'm with you there, Dick."

It was midnight when the Greyhound reached the pier at Woodville.

CHAPTER IV.

RICHARD MAKES A TREMENDOUS SENSATION AT WOODVILLE.

THE mansion at Woodville was dark and silent when Richard stole cautiously up the walk which led from the pier to the house. Of course his father and the other members of the family supposed he was asleep in his chamber, where he had gone at an early hour to retire. He had locked his door as usual, and to make the deception more complete, he had pretended that he was not very well.

His chamber window opened upon the one-story addition which had been erected to afford room for a conservatory. On one end of the structure there was a trellis for the support of a grape vine. After he had locked his door, Richard had opened the window, crawled out upon the roof of the con

servatory, and descended to the ground by the aid
of the trellis.

He intended to return to his room by the same
route, but it was now a more difficult matter than
it had been when the family were all in the sitting
room. Mr. Presby's room was next to his own, and
the old gentleman was not a very sound sleeper.
The difficulty of gaining access to his room was so
great that he was tempted to sleep in the boat
house, and not take the risk of being discovered;
but the condition of his legs, still smarting severely
from the chastisement he had received, would not
permit him to do so. His wounds needed attention, and though he was no surgeon, he knew that
a good washing in cold water, with the application
of a simple remedy he had in his chamber, might
ease the pain, and perhaps save him from serious
consequences.

With a stealthy step he walked round to the
conservatory, and with the utmost care commenced
the ascent of the trellis. With all the precautions
he could use, it was impossible to avoid making some noise, and he trembled lest the wakeful

invalid should hear him. But he succeeded in gaining the roof without creating an alarm. Here he
felt comparatively secure; but sometimes when we
think we are safest we are in the greatest peril.
The roof, wet with the dew of night, was very
slippery; and when he reached up to open the window, his feet flew up beneath him, and he fell,
with noise enough to rouse a deeper sleeper than
Mr. Presby.

"Help! Help! Robbers! Thieves!" shouted the
old gentleman, as he threw open his window.

The invalid's lungs did not seem to be at all
affected, and there would have been no difficulty in
hearing him all over the house, not to say all over
the estate. Richard, taking advantage of the momen-
tary confusion, threw open the window, and sprang
into his room. Doors were opening in all parts
of the house, and he could hear the hurried tread
of the members of the household in the halls.

But Richard did not lose his self-possession, and
hastily threw off his clothes. Placing himself at the
open window, he joined in the cry which Mr. Presby
still continued, and hallooed as lustily as his neigh-

5

bor in the adjoining room. The house was in a
complete uproar, and presently he heard the voices
of his father and uncle Obed at his door.

" Richard," said Mr. Grant.

" Sir," replied the young scapegrace.

" Open the door."

" They are not in here, father; they are out
doors. One of them just jumped off the conservatory, — at least, I think he did."

" Did you see them ?" asked uncle Obed.

" No, I didn't see them, but I think I heard •
them."

Mr. Grant seemed to be satisfied with the information he had gained, and retired from the door.
Richard lighted his lamp, and waited impatiently
for the disturbance to subside; but he had to wait
a long time, for every body about the place had
been thoroughly waked up. Mr. Presby went down
to the sitting room, where, after a thorough search
had been made, the family and the servants had
collected to compare notes, and ascertain to what
extent the supposed robbers had been successful
in their enterprise.

Richard's two sisters, Bertha and Fanny, were
there, and both of them very much terrified. Mr.
Grant soon pacified them with the assurance that
no one had been injured, and that there was no
further danger. But Richard was not there, and his
absence was noticed. He and Mr. Presby had
been the only persons who had heard the robbers,
and they had created the alarm. The old gentleman told his story, and Richard's testimony was
very much needed to complete the chain of evidence. One of the men servants was sent up to
request him to join the party.

"Tell them I don't feel very well, and have
gone to bed again," replied Richard, when the man
delivered his message.

But this was the most dangerous answer he
could have returned; for Mr. Grant, followed by
uncle Obed and Mr. Presby, hastened up stairs to
ascertain the nature of his illness.

"What ails you, Richard?" demanded his father,
in the tones of sympathy and kindness.

"Nothing particular; only I don't feel just
right," replied the young midnight marauder.

terribly alarmed as he thought of the probable
consequences of this visitation.

" Well, open the door, and let me see what I
can do for you," added his father.

" I don't want any thing done. I shall be well
enough in the morning."

" You had better open the door, Richard; I want
to see you about the robbers."

"I can't; I am in bed."

" Don't get up then," said Mr. Grant, more
anxious than at first for the health of his son.   •
" I have a key that will open the door."

These words struck terror to the soul of the
guilty youth, and he sprang out of bed with all
the haste he could command.   One terror filled his
mind — that his father might see his bleeding,
lacerated limbs ; and he did, what guilty persons
often do, the stupidest thing of which the circumstances would admit.   He had blown out the light
when he heard them coming, and now in the darkness he pulled on his pants, forgetting that the
bed clothes would as effectually hide his injured
members as the garment.

He had hardly clothed himself in this partial manner before his father succeeded in opening the door. By the aid of the light which uncle Obed carried, the head and front of the melon expedition was revealed to the visitors, standing in the middle of the room, half clothed and wholly scared.

"Why, Richard! What ails you? Where have you been?" demanded Mr. Grant, as he and the others gazed with astonishment at the sorry figure which the male heir of Woodville presented.

If Richard had attempted to dress himself in the light, he would have rejected the muddy pants he now wore, and consigned them to the deepest depths of the clothes-press. He had rolled in the moist earth of the melon patch, while under the discipline of Mr. Batterman, till his clothes were plastered with mud. His face was begrimed with the rich black mould of the garden, through which the tears of anger and resentment he had shed, under the influence of their natural gravity, had furrowed passages down his cheeks.

In the simple but eloquent language of Mrs. Green, the housekeeper of Woodville, who had fol-

lowed the party up stairs, to offer her services in
the capacity of nurse, Richard was " a sight to
behold." He had retired from the sitting room,
and bade the family good night before nine o'clock,
looking like a decent person. His pants were in
good condition then; certainly, if they had been
in their present plight, it would have been noticed.

The first impulse of the visiting party was to
laugh at the extraordinary appearance he presented;
but a stronger feeling of interest and sympathy
overruled the inclination, and the culprit was spared
this humiliation. Richard was almost as much
astonished as they were, for he had not regarded a
thing so trivial as his personal experience, in the
excitement and terror of the hour.

While the party were scrutinizing him with surprise and anxiety, he happened to glance at the
looking glass on the bureau. Then he saw his
hair tangled and matted with mud and filth; then
he saw his dirty, tear-furrowed cheeks; and then
he saw his befouled and torn pants. In the choice
language of the boys, it seemed to him that " the

cat was out of the bag" beyond the possibility of recovery.

"What ails you, Richard? What under the sun has happened?" asked Mr. Grant again, for the terrified boy made no reply to the first question.

But Richard was an old head, and he had no notion of being defeated in the present contest of words or ideas. He stood like a statue in the middle of the floor, and made no reply to the interrogatories

"Where have you been?" said his father. "Can't you speak?"

"I don't know," replied Richard, with a bewildered look, as he glanced with a vacant stare at his soiled garments.

"Don't know where you have been?"

"No, sir."

"That's very singular," said uncle Obed.

"Have you been up since you went to bed?" demanded Mr. Grant.

"I don't know," replied Richard, vacantly, as though the whole matter was as much a mystery to him as to the others.

" Where were you when the alarm was given ?"

" Out on the roof of the conservatory."

" On the roof !" exclaimed his father.   " How came you there ?"

" I don't know," answered Richard, shaking his head.

" Don't you know any thing about it ?"

" No, sir.   I woke up, and heard some one halloo, Robbers ! thieves !   I was close by the window, and I jumped in, and hallooed with the rest of them."

" Were you standing on the roof ?"

" No, I was flat on my face."

" I see," interposed Mr. Presby, holding up his hands with astonishment, " I understand it all. The poor boy is a sleep walker."

" Richard ?" said Mr. Grant, who had never known his son to do such a thing before.

" Yes, sir ; your boy is unquestionably a somnambulist.   He has been wandering about the garden, and rolling in the mud, in his sleep.   There have been no robbers or thieves here to-night. The poor boy fell on the roof ; that was what waked him up; and the noise of his fall was what caused me to give the alarm."

" Very singular," added uncle Obed.

" I never had any suspicion that he got up in his sleep," said Mr. Grant.

" There are instances on record of persons addicted to the practice who have followed it for years, without discovery. Now, if you will come to my room, I will read you several accounts, given by competent medical authority, of cases just like this," observed Mr. Presby.

But none of the party, at that hour of the night, were disposed to consult the authorities on the subject. If they had looked on the table in Richard's room they might have found there a yellow-covered pamphlet novel, entitled " Sylvester Sound, the Somnambulist." It is a very curious and amusing account of the antics of a sleep-walker, describing the wonderful feats he performed in his slumbers, without having the least idea of what he was doing.

The ingenious young rogue had been reading the book that very day, and in the drama of the " Mid-

night Alarm," played at Woodville, he had chosen
for himself the part of Sylvester Sound. While his
father went for a hammer and nails, to secure the
window, Richard removed his telltale trousers, and
jumped into bed.

CHAPTER V.

RICHARD IS DETERMINED TO BE REVENGED.

MR. GRANT nailed up the window in Richard's room, so that when he should again walk in his sleep, he might not be exposed to the peril of breaking his neck by falling off the roof of the cônservatory. When this important work was accomplished, the party retired. Mr. Presby was a philosopher, and his library had not been a merely ornamental appendage of his house. He had read a great deal, and thought a great deal; and mesmerism, biology, psychology, somnambulism, and kindred subjects, had each in its turn been considered, and a conclusion reached.

Mr. Presby, therefore, was not disposed to return to his bed when the excitement had subsided. So splendid an illustration of the phenomenon of sleep-walking was enough to kindle his enthusiasm. He tried to draw uncle Obed into a discussion on the topic, but the latter was too sleepy. Mr. Grant made a home question of the matter, and did not care to indulge in any philosophical inquiries. One after another the family retired, till the old gentleman was left alone, and then, in despair, he resorted to the " authorities " as he termed his books, and read till the inmates of the hennery began to sound the morning call.

Richard did not come down stairs the next morning till nine o'clock, when Mr. Grant and uncle Obed had both gone to the city. He was so stiff that he could hardly walk ; but he had washed himself clean, and thrown aside the soiled garments he had worn on the expedition.

Already the story of Richard's wonderful doings in his sleep had been circulated all over the estate, and when he limped into the breakfast room, every body supposed he was suffering from the injuries he had received during his nocturnal ramble. Mr. Presby, whose researches were not yet completed, had taken pains to tell the people of the house, that somnambulists were peculiarly sensitive in regard to their involuntary rambles, and, very much to the surprise of Richard, no one even alluded to the events of the night.

There was upon the faces and in the actions of all with whom he came in contact, an expression of abundant sympathy. He was treated with increased kindness and consideration by the family and by the servants. When he had eaten his breakfast, the thought occurred to him that something which might betray him had been left on the Greyhound, and he hastened down to the pier to remove any such evidence.

As he passed the boat house he heard the voices of Mr. Presby and Ben in the building. The former had by no means slept off his enthusiasm in the cause of science; and as soon as the dew was off the grass, he commenced exploring the premises, in search of any appearances that might throw new light upon the conduct of the "poor boy" during his midnight ramble. He recalled the dirty and foul condition of the patient when discovered in his room, and he examined all the vile and filthy places in the neighborhood, for the marks of some terrible struggle that might have taken place between the sleep-walker, and any real or imaginary demon.

The patient seeker after the hidden truths of science had been to the pigsty, to learn whether he had been wrestling with the pigs; he had looked into the cow yard, the horse stables, and the dog kennels for information upon the dark subject; he had patiently explored the cornfield and the potato patch, and every dirty hole he could find; but not a single fact or hint could he obtain to assist him in solving the difficult problem.

In the course of his investigations he had reached the department of Ben, the boatman. He had carefully noted the appearance of the earth on the banks of the river, and, quite fatigued by his unusual exertions, he had seated himself in the boat house, where Ben was at work.

"Have you noticed any thing unusual about the boats, Ben?" asked the old gentleman, after he had given the boatman a full exposition of his views on somnambulism.

"Yes, sir; I noticed that the Greyhound was in

a very dirty, slovenly condition this morning. She wasn't so last night, when I looked at her," replied the boatman.

" Ah, indeed ! "

" The white seats in the standing room were covered with black mud, and upon the edges there were stains of blood."

" Blood ? " queried the philosopher.

" Yes, sir, blood ; I have seen blood in my day, and I know what it looks like."

" Can it be possible ! Blood ! What could have happened to the poor boy ? "

" I don't know, sir."

" It is really awful. There is no knowing what the poor boy may have suffered."

" He got back all right, for the boat was made fast, as usual, to her moorings."

" The poor fellow must have been off somewhere in the boat, in his sleep."

" May be he did, sir," answered Ben, respectfully.

" O, there can be no doubt about it. Isn't it a wonder that he wasn't drowned ? "

"Mr. Richard knows how to handle a boat as well as any boy of his years on the river."

"Yes, but you forget that he was asleep all the time."

"Perhaps he was, sir," said Ben, who did not seem to appreciate Mr. Presby's philosophy.

"But he did not get all that mud and filth upon him while he was in the boat."

"No, sir, of course he didn't; for I wash down the boat every time she is used, and she was as neat as a new pin when I looked into her at sundown last night."

"Then he must have landed somewhere," added the logical Mr. Presby.

"No doubt of that, sir."

"Where do you suppose he landed?"

"I haven't the least idea."

"Do you suppose you could find out by sailing up and down the river, and examining the shore?"

"Well, sir, if you could tell which way the wind is by looking into the ship's coppers, perhaps you might."

"I feel a very deep interest in the poor boy's

welfare," added Mr. Presby, who did not admire Ben's coldness on the subject; "and if you could obtain any information that would throw light on this singular affair, you might confer a great favor on the youth."

" I'll do any thing I can, sir, to find out about it; and if you want to go up and down the river and examine the shore, I'll pull the boat for you."

Mr. Presby accepted this offer, and Richard kept behind the boat house till they had embarked. The roguish author of all these scientific inquiries listened to the old gentleman's remarks on sleep-walking in general, and the phenomena of his own case in particular, till the boat disappeared in the cove above the pier. He then jumped into his skiff, and pulled off to the Greyhound.

Ben had carefully removed all the stains of dirt and blood, and the boat now bore no testimony against him. Whatever the boatman might have thought, he certainly said nothing, and was even willing to countenance Mr. Presby's theory in explanation of the absence of the boat, and of her dirty appearance.

Though Richard had every reason to be satisfied with the success which had attended his representation of the character of a somnambulist, he could not banish the doubts and fears that haunted him. Some unlucky mischance might betray him; " Old Batterbones " or Bates might tell the story; Sandy might be entrapped into an exposure of the affair; indeed, there were so many ways by which the secret might come out, that he was far from satis. fied with the prospect before him.

He was a high-spirited young man, and prided himself upon his healthy body and well-developed muscle, and the idea of being pitied as a person having an infirmity upon him was far from grateful to his sensibilities. He did not much admire Mr. Presby's inquiring mind, and thought he was an " old fool" to trouble himself about what did not concern him. He did not care to be the subject of his meditations. Being watched, pitied, and made the object of a physiological study, were almost as bad as being caught in the act of stealing melons.

But above all considerations of his own safety

or his own comfort was the reflection that he had been whipped — unjustly and cruelly whipped — by such a person as "Old Batterbones." All the bad boys hated and despised him, and he felt that Woodville had been outraged in the person of its male heir. These thoughts rankled in his soul, and he was thirsting for revenge. He was determined to have satisfaction for the injuries that had been heaped upon him. Already the dim outline of a purpose whose execution would secure him ample vengeance was presented to his mind.

While these dark thoughts were passing through his brain, he discovered the boat, with Mr. Presby and Ben, returning to the pier. Not caring to encounter the scrutiny, or answer the questions of the philosopher, he hoisted the sails, and cast off the moorings of the Greyhound. He was anxious to see Sandy Brimblecom, and ascertain whether he had been discovered when he went home. Sailing over to Whitestone, he found Sandy on the wharf, and took him into the boat.

"Did you get into the house all right?" asked Richard as the Greyhound receded from the wharf

"I did, but I got caught for all that. My
mother had missed me, and about one o'clock, after
I had got into bed, the old man came up to my
chamber to see if I was there."

"Of course you pretended to be sound asleep."

"I did; but it wouldn't go down. The old man
asked me where I had been. I told him I had
been over to see you."

"Did you, indeed? ' sneered Richard. "And the
next thing he will do will be to go to my father,
and ask him if you were at our house. My folks
know I went to bed before nine o'clock. You
have got me into a pretty scrape."

"No, I haven't. The old man won't ask any
more questions; but he was mad as thunder with
me for staying out so late. It's all right now, Dick;
you needn't give yourself any trouble about it."

"I shall not do that, whatever happens."

Richard then described the happy "dodge" by
which he had thrown dust in the eyes of all the
inmates of Woodville. Sandy was much amused
at the account, and expressed a decided admiration
for the wonderful genius of his companion, and

even went so far as to request the loan of the remarkable work which had suggested the expedient. He would like to read that book, though he was not in the habit of doing such things.

"See there, Sandy," said Richard, as he pulled up his pants, and exhibited to his friend the wales and broken skin upon his legs.

"That's hard," replied Sandy, as he shook his head. "The old villain laid it on well."

"He did, and he shall pay dearly for it," added Richard, as he compressed his lips and ground his teeth. "I'll be revenged upon him if it costs me my life."

"I'm with you there, Dick."

"It shall be the worst night's work for Old Batterbones that ever he did."

"What are you going to do, Dick?"

"Will you stand by me, Sandy?" demanded Richard, earnestly.

"Certainly; to be sure I will. But, Dick, we mustn't burn our own fingers," said his prudent companion. "What are you going to do?"

In low tones, Richard detailed the scheme into wnich his outline of a purpose had grown, and when they parted at noon, the arrangements were all completed.

CHAPTER VI.

RICHARD GIVES ANOTHER ILLUSTRATION OF
SLEEP—WALKING.

For six or seven nights following the expedition to the watermelon patch of Mr. Batterman, Richard Grant did not " walk in his sleep." The parental solicitude of his father prompted him to set a watch for several nights; and Mr. Presby, who was still anxious to pursue his scientific investigations, slept with one eye open, that he might be in readiness to avail himself of the reappearance of the phenomenon.

The philosopher's hint that sleep-walkers are sensitive to any allusion to their infirmity, had prevented him and Mr. Grant from informing the subject of their precautions of the steps they had taken to observe his movements, and Richard was entirely unconscious that vigilant eyes were

upon him while he slept, or while he ought to
sleep.

But Richard was too lame and sore from the
effects of his flogging to indulge again so soon in
the luxury of "sleep-walking." He had not been
questioned in regard to the blood upon the seats
of the Greyhound, for, being asleep when the stains
were made, of course he would know nothing
about them. Mr. Presby explained his inactivity
and want of energy upon philosophical principles,
and every body seemed to be satisfied.

The salve which the sufferer applied to his
wounded members healed the bruises in a few
days, and he was again in condition to pursue his
wonted sports and pleasures. After the lapse of a
week, as the patient exhibited no further signs of
the malady, the watch was discontinued; but Mr.
Presby was too enthusiastic in the cause of science
to abandon the case so soon. He sat up in his
chamber till midnight, with his ears wide open, to
catch the slightest indication of a movement on the
part of his interesting subject.

Every day, Richard and Sandy met; and they

never failed to renew the mutual pledges they had made to be revenged upon " Old Batterbones." The plan was discussed and amended till no further improvement could be made ; and by this time Richard was so far recovered from his injuries as to enable him to take the leading part in its execution. The night was appointed for the purpose, and it was agreed that the boys should meet at a point just below Whitestone, where Richard was to take Sandy into the Greyhound, and proceed to the inlet where they had before landed.

It was a very difficult matter for Richard to get out of the house without detection. If he could succeed in opening his door, and walk through the long halls of the mansion without attracting the attention of any of its numerous inmates, he could hardly expect to unlock any of the outer doors with safety. After much reflection, he decided that it would be the better way to go out as he had gone before — over the roof of the conservatory, and down the trellis.

With the proper tools, therefore, he had removed the nails with which his father had secured the window of his chamber. He had then skilfully adjusted them, so that they appeared to be as his father had left them, though he could easily pull them out. At ten o'clock he retired as usual, but the hour of meeting was one o'clock, for the young rascals had come to the conclusion that their purpose could be better executed in the small hours of the morning, when the farmer and his man would probably be asleep.

Richard waited impatiently till he heard the clock strike twelve. There had been no noise in the chamber of Mr. Presby for some time, and he concluded that the old gentleman must be asleep. He had gone to bed as usual, in order to remove any suspicion in case he should find it necessary to act the part of the sleep-walker again. He rose and dressed himself for the expedition, using the utmost care to avoid disturbing the slumbers of the troublesome philosopher in the adjoining room.

Every thing worked to his entire satisfaction, and he was not conscious that he had made the slightest noise. The nails were removed from the window ; but, though he had taken the precaution to oil the sash where it slid up and down, it creaked a little, in spite of all the care he could use. He was satisfied that the noise could not wake Mr. Presby, and he continued his operations. Leaving the window open, as a somnambulist would naturally be expected to do, he crept softly over the roof, and reached the trellis without accident.

As yet there was no appearance of an interruption; but the first bar of the trellis, upon which he placed his foot, creaked and snapped. As the noise, so far as he could see, attracted no notice, he resumed his attempt, and reached the ground without any further impediment, real or imaginary.

With stealthy step he retreated from the house till there was no longer any danger of being discovered. Quickening his pace, he soon reached the pier, and with the skiff boarded the Greyhound. The night was certainly favorable for the execution of dark deeds. The midnight assassin, the incendiary, or the burglar would have rejoiced in its darkness, its dense black clouds, and its fitful winds.

Richard Grant still felt the cowhide of his enemy

tingling upon his legs, and still felt its iron pier-
cing his soul. The injury he had received a week
before, rankled in his bosom as it had the hour
after it had been inflicted. Neither the time that
had elapsed, nor the peril attending his present
enterprise, in any degree moderated the spirit of
revenge that burned in his soul.

As soon as he had secured the skiff at the buoy
to which the sail boat was moored, he opened the
door of the stern locker, and drew forth a small
bottle. He shook it to satisfy himself that the
contents were safe, and then restored it to the
place from which he had taken it. He then examined his pockets to assure himself that some
other article necessary for his purpose was all right.
No mistakes or omissions had been made, and he
proceeded to hoist the mainsail. He then cast off
the moorings, and hoisted the jib. The wind was
too fresh to permit the Greyhound to carry all sail,
and even with what he had set, she put her rail
under the water at the first forward impulse.

One less skilful and courageous than Richard
would have been terrified by the fierce waves and

the gloom of the night, especially if bound upon an errand of evil and crime; but he held the tiller with a steady hand, and heeded not the spray that broke upon the half-deck of the Greyhound. A few moments in such a breeze were sufficient to carry him over the river to the place of rendezvous. The point was as familiar to him as the pier at Woodville; and as soon as he could obtain a view of the dark outline of the shore, he ran the boat alongside the point, with as little difficulty as though it had been broad daylight.

Sandy Brimblecom was not there, and an expression of anger escaped from the lips of Richard, when he found that the partner of his iniquitous scheme might possibly fail him. He gave the signal whistle with which they were in the habit of calling each other; but there was no reply. The clocks on the churches in Whitestone struck one, and Richard waited half an hour after he heard them — half an hour, which seemed like half a day to him.

He was afraid that Sandy's heart had failed him, or that his father had discovered him; and Rich-

ard decided to proceed alone with the enterprise.
Disgusted at the failure of his associate, he pushed
off from the point. As he did so, he discovered
another boat a short distance up the river, moving
off from the shore. He watched it for a moment,
till it disappeared in the gloom. It was not a
common thing to see sail boats out at such an
hour, and on such a night as this was; but he
concluded that it was some gardener taking his
produce to an early market, and he gave himself
no uneasiness.

Just as he lost sight of the boat, he heard the
familiar whistle of Sandy. Putting the Greyhound
about, he ran under the lee of the point, and his
friend leaped on board. Richard immediately put
off again, and shaped the course of the boat for
the inlet near the garden of " Old Batterbones."

" You are late, Sandy," said Richard, in reproach-
ful tones.

" Can't help it. I got asleep, and didn't wake
up," replied Sandy, with a long gape.

"Asleep! What did you go to sleep for? I
haven't been asleep."

"I didn't mean to, but I was so sleepy I couldn't help it."

"You came pretty near spoiling your share of the fun. I had just cast off, and was going to put the thing through alone."

"I wish you had," answered Sandy, in a tone which did not please his companion any better than the words themselves.

"What do you mean?"

"It's a bad scrape we are getting into, and I wish we were well out of it. If I hadn't promised to go, I wouldn't have any thing to do with it."

"Old Batterbones licked you as well as me."

"I know that, and I should like to pay him off for it; but I don't believe it will do to go in quite so steep as we are going."

"You are chicken-hearted, Sandy. I thought you had more grit than that."

"I think I have got as much as you have, but I don't believe it will pay to rub your nose on a grindstone. Your nose will get the worst of it."

"You can back out, if you want to," added Richard, in an indifferent tone.

" I don't want to back out. I agreed to go,
and I am going, if I have to be hung for it. I
only say, it is a bad scrape."

" No scrape at all, Sandy. I don't calculate to
get found out."

" You didn't calculate to before, but you did;
and Old Batterbones got more fun out of the
scrape than you did. Perhaps he will this time."

" If you are afraid, Sandy, back out, and we
will go home again."

" I'm not afraid : don't use that word to me
again, Dick. If I had been afraid, I shouldn't
come, of course."

By this time the Greyhound was off the little
inlet, near Mr. Batterman's garden, and, as a matter of prudence, all conversation was suspended.
The boat shot into the inlet, and was made fast to
the same tree as on the former occasion. As the
business of these hopeful youths was not with the
melon patch, they took a different road this time.

They had gone but a short distance before the
rushing of a boat through the water was heard.
They paused and Richard saw a sail, which he

believed he had seen before that night, pass by the mouth of the inlet. He caught but a glance of it, as it cut a tangent along the small circle of his vision.

" I don't like the looks of that boat, Sandy," whispered Richard, as the sail disappeared in the gloom.

" Why not ? "

" What is any one sailing about the river at this time of night for ? "

" I don't know," added Sandy, who did not seem to be at all alarmed at the appearance of the boat.

" I think I have seen her before to-night," continued Richard.

" If you are afraid, we will both back out, and then neither can twit the other."

" I'm not afraid ; come along. I've no notion of backing out." And Richard moved on, followed by his reluctant associate.

When they had ascended the hill, they carefully walked all over the grounds to satisfy themselves that the farmer and his man were not keeping vigil over the melons ; but they could neither see nor hear any thing that betokened the presence of a human being. Satisfied with this survey of the ground, Richard led the way to the barn, where he had received his terrible flagellation. The memories of the place were not pleasant, and they intensified the hatred he bore the owner of the premises, and fanned the flame of vengeance that was burning in his soul.

The barn was an old building, and very much out of repair. It contained the farmer's horses and oxen, his wagons, his hay, and other produce. On the side nearest to the river, some of the boards had been forced partly off by the pressure of the hay; and against one of these places Richard sat down upon the ground.

"Pull out some of the hay, Sandy," whispered Richard, as he drew from his pocket the bottle which he had taken from the locker of the boat.

Sandy hinted something about backing out again; but a sneer from Richard silenced him, and he obeyed the order. While he was doing so, Richard walked round the barn to satisfy himself that no one was near. They were alone, and the wicked work proceeded.

CHAPTER VII.

RICHARD KINDLES A LITTLE FIRE.

SANDY continued to pull out the hay from behind the board, till Richard, who, as engineer,
conducted the operations, directed him to suspend
his labors. The contents of the bottle were poured
upon the heap of loose hay.

" What's that, Dick ?" asked Sandy.

" Spirits of turpentine. I intend to make sure
work of it," answered Richard.

" I wouldn't use that stuff," added Sandy.

" Why not ? "

" To tell the truth, Dick, I was in hopes the
fire wouldn't burn."

" I believe you are a fool, Sandy Brimblecom !
Have you come clear over here, in the dead of the
night, to kindle a fire that will not burn ? "

" I don't like the idea of setting the barn on

fire," whispered Sandy, in an earnest tone. "What do you suppose they will do with us, if we should get found out?"

"We shall not get found out."

"We shall be sent to the state prison—at least 1 shall."

"I shall, if you are; we shall both be in the same boat, and if one goes down the other must."

"I don't know about that," said Sandy; "your father is rich, and he will get you off. I shall have to stand all the racket."

"Shut up, Sandy! I have gone too far to back out now," added Richard, decidedly, as he took a bunch of matches from his pocket.

"Hold on a moment, Dick, before it is too late. It will be cheaper to do our thinking now than it will be after the barn is burned down."

"I have done all the thinking I care to do already. The die is cast, Sandy. I won't back out now, and you shall not."

"It's too bad to burn up the horses and oxen in the barn. That's cruel. If it wasn't for them, I wouldn't say a word."

" Very well; we will go round and turn out the horses and oxen. I don't want to burn them any more than you do."

" But the noise will wake the farmer and his man."

" No, it won't. I have thought a great deal about the animals, and it goes right against my grain to hurt them, especially the horses."

" I don't want to burn the barn, any way."

" You are a coward and a fool, Sandy."

" It's easy enough for you to say so, when you know your father has money enough to buy up Old Batterbones, if we get into any scrape."

" Come, no more whining, Sandy; I'm going to get the horses and oxen out, and then I'm going to burn the barn."

" I'm off, then."

" Very good; but if I get into trouble, I will blow on you."

This consideration staggered Sandy, and he concluded to stay and see the end of the wicked enterprise. The house of Mr. Batterman was at a considerable distance from the barn, and there

was but little danger that the humane policy of
the young incendiaries would expose them to any
additional peril.

Richard, followed by Sandy, entered the barn,
and turned all the animals loose. They drove
them into a lot where they could not get near the
fire. The only thing that had weighed upon the
mind of the broker's son, in the prosecution of
his mad enterprise, was now removed, and he returned to the place where he had prepared the
materials for starting the conflagration. Again
Sandy stated his objections, and urged Richard to
abandon the scheme ; but the latter, without any
reply to this remonstrance, drew a card of matches
across a stone, and applied the burning mass to
the hay which had been saturated with turpentine.

The heap of combustible matter suddenly blazed
up, lighting all the fields around them. The work
had been surely done, and it was too late for Sandy
to urge any more of his objections.

" Come, Sandy, the work is done. Now use
your legs," said Richard, as he started at the top of
his speed towards the inlet where the Greyhound lay.

Sandy's legs did not fail him on this emergency, for he soon outstripped his companion. They had gone but a few rods, when both were appalled at the discovery of two men, who were running towards the fire with all their might — which was not saying much, for both of them seemed to be old and stiff, and incapable of making very good time even on so pressing an emergency as the present.

The guilty boys were filled with terror. The shock was so great that it seemed to deprive them of their strength, and they found their legs giving out under them.

"We are caught, Dick," gasped Sandy, when he could regain breath enough to speak.

"No, we are not; come along. Don't stop here," answered Richard, who was beginning to recover his self-possession.

They ran as fast as their weakened limbs would permit, till they reached the bank of the river. Richard jumped into the boat and hoisted the sails, while Sandy cast off the painter, and they were soon standing out from the shore before the fresh breeze. Neither of them spoke for some minutes.

for neither of them had breath enough left in his
body to do so.

"The fire don't burn," said Richard, when the
boat had gone far enough to enable him to see
over the high bank of the river.

"Don't it?" asked Sandy, hoarsely, for the terror and exhaustion of the awful moments through
which he had just passed seemed to have choked
up his throat, and deprived him of his voice.

"No; it is as dark, up there as it was before
we landed."

"I am glad of it," gasped Sandy, who was beginning to breathe a little easier.

"I'm not," added Richard, firmly. "We shall
only have the job to do over again."

"If you ever catch me in such a scrape as this
again, you may let me know it when you do."

"You might as well have the game as the
name."

"I don't know about that. I am glad the barn
didn't burn. Are you sure the fire has gone out?"

"No doubt of it. There isn't enough to light
your cigar."

"I suppose those men put it out. Who do you think they were?"

"I don't know, and I don't care. I wish they had been somewhere else. They have spoiled my night's work."

"I am glad they have; and I thank them with all my heart for what they have done."

"I don't; you might as well be hung for an old sheep as a lamb. If we are caught it will be all the same with us as though we had burned the barn."

"Who do you suppose the men were?"

"I haven't the least idea. I don't care."

"Yes, you do care, Dick. What's the use of talking in that way? You don't want to be found out any more than I do."

"I know that, but we are not found out; and that isn't all — we shall not be."

"I should like to be satisfied on that point."

"The men didn't take any notice at all of us, and I am certain they did not see us."

"They couldn't help seeing us, Dick. The fire

8 *

lit up the whole field, so that it was as light as broad day."

"Suppose they did see us; they couldn't tell who we were. Keep a stiff upper lip, Sandy, and it will be all right."

"I can only hope for the best, but I shall be scared at my own shadow for a month to come," added Sandy, in whose nature a vein of candor appeared to be suddenly developed, for he was not in the habit of acknowledging that he was afraid of any thing.

"You don't talk a bit like Sandy Brimblecom," sneered Richard; "and you act more like an old woman than a fellow of any spunk."

"Humph! I'll bet you are as scared as I am, only you won't own it."

"I don't know what fear means, Sandy."

"O, you can brag; but when a fellow can go and set a man's barn afire, without wincing, he's worse than I am; that's all I've got to say."

"Worse than you are!" said Richard. "Didn't you agree to the whole thing? Didn't you go in

for paying off Old Batterbones? Didn't you come
down here to burn the barn with me?"

" I did, but I didn't want to come."

" What did you come for, then?"

" Because I agreed to come."

" You're not the fellow I took you to be. You
joined me in the affair, and then, at the last moment, you begin to whine like a sick monkey."

" I'm not so far gone that I can burn a man's
barn without feeling it."

" You haven't got the pluck of a mosquito."

" You've said about enough on that tack, Dick
Grant," replied Sandy, who did not relish the reflections cast upon his courage.

" I shall say what I think best."

" No, you won't! I'm sorry for what I've done,
and I'm willing to own it; but I won't take any
sauce from you or any other fellow."

" You can talk big enough," sneered Richard

" Shut up, or I'll bat you over the head."

" Humph!"

" Just put me ashore, Dick Grant, and you and
I will part company."

" I'm willing."

Both boys felt that enough had been said, and
the conversation was discontinued by mutual consent. Richard, notwithstanding his bravado, was
no better satisfied with himself than Sandy. Though
he had spoken of " doing the job over again," he
had not the slightest idea of repeating the experi-
ment. The shock which the discovery of the two
men had given him, was too much even for his
strong nerves ; and though he was not willing to
confess it, he was sorry for what he had done.
The terror of being found out had damped the
spirit of revenge. The excitement of the affair had
passed away, and like his companion in wickedness, visions of public trial, of the house of cor-
rection, or the state prison, began to flit before him.

He was not sorry that the barn had been saved
from destruction ; and the only pleasant reflection
in connection with the whole transaction was, that
he had insisted upon saving the horses and the
oxen. It was with Richard as it is with all who
commit crimes. They are led on by the spirit of
revenge, or some other strong motive. There is a

kind of excitement which urges them on till the wicked deed is committed. Then the criminal excitement subsides; the hour of reflection comes, burdened also with the fear of discovery. To some extent, crime is its own punishment; at least, it is so with those who have not become hardened in iniquity.

Richard brought the Greyhound up to the point where he had taken Sandy on board. He did not like to part with him in anger, for, to a certain extent, he sympathized with him in his penitential confession. But, more than this, he was afraid Sandy might revenge himself upon him for the reproaches he had uttered.

"Let's not quarrel, Sandy," said Richard, as he laid the boat alongside the landing place.

"I don't want to quarrel, but I won't be picked upon by you," replied Sandy, with spirit.

"I'll take it all back. Let's be friends again. We have failed to do what we intended, and perhaps it will be just as well for us."

"I'm glad you are coming to your senses. Do you mean to try it again?"

" We won't burn the barn, Sandy, but we must
pay off Old Batterbones in some other way."

" I'll do it. I'll hook his apples, pull out the
linchpins of his wagon, throw a dead cat into his
well, or any thing of that sort, with you, but I
won't attempt to burn any man's barn again. No,
never ! "

" We'll fix him yet, Sandy. When shall I see
you again ? "

" I shall be round the wharf to-morrow."

" I'll see you there. Good night to you, Sandy."

" Good night, Dick."

Boys don't usually bid each other good night
after they have been doing wicked deeds ; and
Richard's parting salutation was a peace-offering,
rather than the kindly wish of a friend.

Sandy made his way up to Whitestone, and
Richard again pushed off upon the troubled
waters of the Hudson. The Greyhound leaped over
the waves as though she was in haste to get out
of the disgraceful business in which she had been
employed. Richard heard the clocks in Whitestone

striking three, as he grappled his moorings and made fast to them.

He landed from the skiff, and, like a thief in the night, stole up to his father's house. Before he attempted to ascend the trellis, he pulled off his boots, and fastening them together with his handkerchief, slung them around his neck. He reached the roof of the conservatory without noise, and then, to his utter consternation, discovered a light in Mr. Presby's room. But the precaution he had taken in the removal of his boots enabled him to reach his chamber window without producing a sound. Then, to his astonishment and terror, he found that the window he had left open was closed.

Some one had been there.

CHAPTER VIII.

RICHARD BEHOLDS HOW GREAT A MATTER A LIT-
TLE FIRE KINDLETH.

THE window of the chamber was not fastened, and when Richard gained admission, he found the door locked as he had left it. The window must therefore have been closed from the outside; but this did not seem probable, and he came to the conclusion that the sash had dropped of itself. This was a very comforting reflection, and it removed many of the doubts and fears which disturbed him.

Congratulating himself upon his escape from manifold perils by land and water, Richard undressed himself and went to bed. But tired as he was, he could not go to sleep for some time. His brain was busy calculating the chances of detection, and devising schemes to avert suspicion if any should be fastened upon him. Nature triumphed at last, and he went to sleep.

Late the next morning, when he went down stairs, he was pale and haggard. Somewhat to his surprise, he found that his father had not gone to the city as usual. Every body looked sober, and Mr. Grant's face wore a very stern and troubled expression. Richard ate his breakfast in silence, wondering all the time what so many serious and averted faces portended.

"You were out again last night, Richard," said his father, when they met in the sitting room at a later hour.

"No, sir, not that I am aware of," replied Richard, with as much self-possession as he could call to his aid, though his heart was leaping with fear and anxiety.

"If you had been out, shouldn't you have been aware of it?" asked his father, fixing a penetrating gaze upon him.

"I don't know. I only judge by what happened the other night," answered Richard, who had determined to "run" the sleep-walking expedient again.

9

"You mean by that you got up in your sleep
if you got up at all?"

"Yes, sir."

"You were entirely unconscious when you got
up the other night and went off in the Greyhound
— were you?"

"Of course I was."

A faint smile played upon the lips of Mr. Grant,
while the faces of uncle Obed and Mr. Presby wore
a decidedly comical expression. Though Richard
could not see "where the laugh came in," he was
conscious that he had placed himself in a ludicrous
attitude.

"And you were asleep last night when you went
out — were you?" continued Mr. Grant.

"If I went out, I suppose I was," replied Richard,
going to the window and looking out, thus turning
his back to those in the room.

He could not bear the penetrating gaze of his
father, and the quizzing glances of Mr. Presby and
uncle Obed were utterly insupportable.

"Mr. Presby, you have devoted considerable
attention to the phenomena of sleep-walking,"

added uncle Obed. "What do you think of this case?"

"I think it is the most remarkable one on record," replied the philosopher, whose smile had grown into a broad grin. "Richard, I am deeply interested in the investigation of this matter, and I want to ask you a few questions. Will you oblige me by answering them?"

"I will if I can," said Richard, rather doggedly, for he was fully satisfied, by this time, that the old gentleman was quizzing him.

"If you *can*, then, will you be kind enough to tell me whether Sandy Brimblecom was asleep or not, when he joined you in the boat at the point below Whitestone?"

"Who? Sandy joined me?" stammered Richard, staggered by this home thrust of the friend of the family.

"Yes; I am very anxious to know whether there is a sympathy between sleep-walkers which draws them together, even though separated by miles of space."

Richard made no reply; he had none to make.

He had no idea how much his tormentors knew of the events of the night.

"You don't answer, my boy. I have been tho butt of your uncle for the last week on account of my devotion to the cause of science. I have studied your case very thoroughly, and I may want to make a report of it to the scientific associations."

"Why don't you answer him, Dick?" added uncle Obed, who, notwithstanding the serious character of the matter, could not restrain his laughter at the ludicrous side of the question.

"I don't care about your making fun of me," replied the poor somnambulist.

"My dear boy, this is a scientific, a physiological investigation. You pulled out the nails which your father had driven into the window; you skulked away from the house; you went down to your boat, got under way in a squally, dark night, and met another sleep-walker on the other side of the river;—I presume he was asleep, for you do not say to the contrary;—you sailed down the river to a certain inlet; you landed, and went up to Mr. Batterman's barn; you removed the horses and oxen from it;

you poured turpentine upon a bunch of loose hay prepared for the purpose; you lighted your matches and set fire to it; and all the while you were fast asleep. And you returned home and went to bed again without waking. Really, my dear boy, this is tne most astonishing case of somnambulism on record. I have vainly looked over my books for a parallel instance. Can you tell me what your dreams were last night? Did you dream any thing of this kind?"

Richard was filled with dismay at this recital of the events of the night. The mysterious boat he had twice seen was the only explanation of the minuteness of Mr. Presby's details that suggested itself to his mind.

"You talked quite rationally in your sleep, which is a new development in somnambulism. But, after all," continued the devotee of science, "the phenomena of last night were not near so remarkable as those of the former occasion. By the way, my dear boy, do sleep-walkers have any particular fondness for watermelons?"

Uncle Obed laughed outright at this sally, and

9 *

even Mr. Grant, wounded as his paternal heart was by the discovery, could not help smiling, though he felt more like weeping than laughing.

"You are silent, my dear boy," resumed Mr. Presby. "This is an important physiological inquiry, and you would enlarge the sphere of human knowledge of this interesting subject, if you would answer me."

Richard was inclined to get into a passion, but the consciousness of his guilt restrained him, and he listened in silence to the satirical remarks of the old gentleman.

"But the most astounding fact of all is, that you could take such an unmerciful flogging as Mr. Batterman gave you without waking up," continued the inquisitor. "Perhaps you did wake under this cruel infliction, but went to sleep again when the castigation was over. Can you inform me on this point?"

"You have made fun enough of me," replied Richard; but his words were very tame, considering the amount of provocation he had endured.

"Were you asleep, Richard, on these two nights

when you have been prowling about the neighborhood?" demanded his father, sternly.

"No, sir, I was not," said Richard, to whom the
ridicule of Mr. Presby and uncle Obed was more
terrible than any punishment he could receive for
his misdeeds.

"I am glad to see you have some honesty left
in your composition. You acknowledge the deception, and we will let the farce end here. You
have become a thief and a midnight incendiary.
I have been weak and indulgent towards you.
My eyes are opened, and I shall pursue a different
course."

Mr. Grant's lip trembled with emotion as he
spoke. Mr. Presby and uncle Obed suddenly became very serious, and it was plain to the culprit
that the farce had really ended.

"Richard, I knew you were wild, and even dissolute, but I did not think you would steal," added
Mr. Grant, with deep feeling.

"It was only for fun, father," pleaded Richard.

"Do you practise the trade of the incendiary for
fun?" asked his father, sternly.

"That was only because Mr. Batterman flogged me. He had no business to do that."

"And so you would burn his barn?"

"I didn't burn it."

"It would have burned to the ground, if Mr. Presby and Ben had not put the fire out. I have let my friend expose you in his own way, because the trouble he has taken reveals to me your true character. You are worse than your dissolute companions. Richard, you have become a villain!"

Mr. Grant rose from his chair and walked away to hide the tears which this sad revelation of his son's character drew from his eyes.

"He is not so bad as he might be," interposed Mr. Presby. "Remember that he saved the animals in the barn."

"The record is black even with this redeeming line," said Mr. Grant. "I would rather follow my son to his grave than have him become such a wretch as you are, Richard. Shall I let you take the consequences of your crime?"

"What consequences, father?" asked Richard, with a degree of humility he had never before exhibited

"Are you a simpleton? Don't you know the penalty of your crime?"

"We didn't burn the barn."

"In the eye of the law you are just as guilty as though the barn had burned to the ground. If convicted, you would be sent to the state prison. I have made up my mind what to do with you," said Mr. Grant, as he walked out of the room, for his emotions would no longer permit him to re-main.

"You have got into a bad scrape, Dick," added uncle Obed, as he shook his head, and followed his brother, leaving the culprit alone with Mr. Presby.

"He will not let them send me to the state prison?" said Richard, fearful that his father might have abandoned all hope of redeeming him from the error of his ways.

"You have been a very bad boy," replied Mr. Presby.

"I am very sorry for it, and I mean to do better."

"I hope you will, my dear boy. Your father

has suffered terribly since I returned, and poor
Bertha has dcne nothing but weep for the last two
hours.   You are ruining yourself and wounding
the hearts of your friends more than words can
describe."

"I will try to do better."

"Your father will not trust you again."

"What is he going to do?"

"He will inform you himself," replied Mr.
Presby, as he withdrew from the room.

Richard was alone with his own thoughts and
fears.   He felt as though his career had reached
its close, though he could not imagine what terrible thing his father intended to do.   He was really
sorry for what he had done, whether his sorrow
was caused by a genuine feeling that he had done
wrong, or by the fear of punishment.

His mind was in a confused state; the past with
its sorrows, and the future with its terrors, whirled
through his brain.   He wanted time for reflection,
and leaving the house, he walked down to the pier
to deliberate upon the situation.

Ben was there, and Richard began to question him,

for Mr. Presby had intimated that the boatman was
with him the night before. From him he learned
all the facts in regard to their movements. It appeared that the old gentleman had heard Richard
when he opened the window, and had watched him
closely, fully satisfied, however, that he was asleep.

When Mr. Presby, from the roof of the conservatory, had noted the direction he took, he had
closed the window, and called the boatman to assist him. They had followed him in the large sail
boat, and landed near the point where Sandy was
taken on board the Greyhound. By this time,
Ben's original idea that Richard was wide awake
was adopted by Mr. Presby. By the exercise of
great skill and caution, they had kept near the
boys, and had put out the fire almost as soon as it
was kindled.

While they were still on the ground, Mr. Batterman, who had been awakened by the bright
light of the burning hay, made his appearance.
He found the two old men in the very act of putting out the fire. Mr. Presby smothered the
flames by throwing his great-coat upon it.

"Now, Mr. Richard," continued the boatman, "Mr. Presby saved you. He was acquainted with Batterman, and has a mortgage on his farm. The farmer suspected who had attempted to burn his building; he laid it to you at once, and told us all about the scrape when you stole the melons. You don't know how mad he was, Mr. Richard. But Mr. Presby made it all right with him, and he promised not to prosecute. Mr. Richard, you had better not walk in your sleep any more."

Richard did not like this last remark, and he walked down the pier. The state prison was only a bugbear then; but his father meant to do something. He was about to get into his skiff to visit the Greyhound when Ben hailed him.

"My orders are, not to let you have any of the boats," said he.

The new order of things had begun, and he returned to the house. His father was in the sitting room when he entered.

"Richard," said Mr. Grant, "to-morrow you will leave home for some months. I have decided to place you in a boarding school, where you will be under the eye of one who is competent to manage you."

This was the great matter which a little fire had kindled.

10

CHAPTER IX.

RICHARD GOES TO THE TUNBROOK MILITARY INSTITUTE.

RICHARD had several times before been threat-ened with a residence at a boarding school. Most of his education had been obtained at home, under the superintendence of tutors, and special teachers in various branches. He had been under little or no restraint; and the consequence was, that his mental discipline had been very imperfect, and his stock of knowledge was small, considering the op-portunities he had enjoyed.

His father had long been conscious of his de-ficiencies, and proposed to send him to a boarding school, for the benefit of its discipline; but Rich-ard was so averse to the idea, that his father had from time to time postponed his departure. When Mr. Grant saw his son associating with bad boys he again proposed to send him, and had actually sought out a suitable place for him; but his own financial trials and troubles had prevented him from executing his purpose.

If Richard's education had failed to develop his intellect in an adequate degree, it had built up a sound and vigorous constitution. Riding on horseback, sailing and rowing, had been pastimes for which he had sacrificed intellectual culture. But there was still time to remedy this deficiency, for the youth was hardly sixteen.

The establishment which Mr. Grant had selected for the future residence of his son was the Tunbrook Military Institute, under the superintendence of Colonel Brockridge. This place had been chosen, not because it was a military institution, but because its principal was a thorough disciplinarian. He had the reputation of being a just and fair man, and was very popular with boys of strong constitution and decisive temperaments. No "milk-and-water" boys were ever sent to him; or, if they were, they soon left the Institute, or became vigorous and decided in their habits.

Colonel Brockridge had been in the army, though his title was won in the militia. He was a thorough teacher, and was conscientious and faithful in the discharge of his duties to those who were intrusted to his care. He was a " positive man," and no fear of what the father or mother would say or do ever induced him to alter his plans, or change his purposes.

Though the Institute was conducted on military principles, it was not peculiarly the school of the soldier. The principal believed in discipline; this was his hobby; and he believed that he could best secure system and order by adopting military routine. His success justified his theory. He had more applicants than he had places.

Richard knew all about the Tunbrook Military Institute. He had carefully read its circular, and its rules and regulations. They did not suit him. He was not a devotee of discipline, in its application to himself. He was very impatient of restraint, as the reader has already seen, and he did not like the idea of being sent to this Institute.

When his father had given him his final sentence,

he retired to his chamber. The shame which attended the discovery of his guilt still rested heavily
upon him, and he was in a more humble and
tractable mood than usual. Under ordinary circumstances he would have rebelled against the decision
of his father. He would have frightened his sister
by threatening to run away to sea. It is true, this
thought occurred to him on the present occasion;
but Ben had told him enough about the life of a
sailor to convince him that he should not improve
his condition by such a course.

There seemed to be no alternative but passive
obedience. He did not want to go, but he felt
that his father must certainly conquer if he attempted
to resist. He had always had his own way to a
very great extent. He had always been a conqueror
himself — at least he felt so, and he could not endure the thought of being compelled to yield im-
plicit obedience to any person.

At this time Richard's thoughts took a peculiar
turn. The shame he endured, the reproaches that
had been heaped upon him, caused him to feel
that there was something wanting in his character.

The path in which he had been travelling, for the
first time in his life seemed to lead to destruction.
When he considered that he had been detected in
the act of stealing, and of setting fire to a barn,
and in practising a gross and wicked deception, he
felt that his road was down hill; that he should
become a dissolute and worthless man.

He was sitting on the stool of repentance. From
a prudential penitence he had arrived at a genuine one. Something must be done. There was
something to be conquered. There was a harder
battle before him than any he had yet fought.
He was master of the boats, of the horses, of the
servants, and even of his companions at Whitestone; but there was one whom he had never
conquered — one that held him in leading-strings,
and was pulling him down to ruin and destruction.

He must conquer himself.

Richard had had such thoughts as these before,
but they had never seemed so substantial as now.
He felt the necessity of reforming his life and
character — of conquering himself, his greatest enemy. As he looked upon his dissolute course, upon

the events of the preceding night, and its fellow a week before, he was disgusted with himself, and wondered how he could so easily embrace his besetting sin.

While he was engaged in these reflections, his sister Bertha entered his chamber. She had heard of the sentence, and she had come to comfort him. Her eyes were still red with weeping, for she had almost lost hope of the reform of her brother.

" I have been trying to see you for the last two hours," said she, as she sat down by his side.

" Don't cry any more, Berty," said he, with unwonted tenderness.

" I will try not to do so, Richard. Father says you are going away to-morrow."

" Yes, Berty, 1 suppose I am," replied he, with an appearance of resignation.

" I shall miss you very much."

" It will be a good miss — won't it ? "

" Why, Richard ! You don't think so — do you ? "

" Well, I have been a kind of nuisance to you."

" No, Richard ; don't say that."

" I have been in all sorts of scrapes."

"I would a great deal rather have you stay at home, and — and — "

"And be a good boy," added Richard.

"That's what I mean, Richard."

"Berty, I think I have sowed all my wild oats now."

"I hope so."

"I suppose I have been a very bad boy," said he, with a kind of deprecating smile, as though he did not believe more than one half he said.

"It was all those bad boys you went with; if it hadn't been for them, you would have done very well. That Sandy Brimblecom hasn't done you any good."

"I hope I haven't done him any hurt, Berty. I won't be mean, when I get into trouble. I don't think Sandy is any worse than I am. I don't know but that he is a little better. I suppose he and I must part company now."

"It will be all for the best."

"Berty, I am off to-morrow. I have given you a great deal of trouble. I mean to do better. I am going to turn over a new leaf."

"O, I hope so, Richard!"

"I mean so, this time."

"I am so glad!"

"Don't you think father will let me stay at home, if I do well?"

"Perhaps he will."

"I don't like the idea of being put into a strait jacket, and tied to a bell rope."

"It would be hard for you."

"I can't stand it, any how. I have made up my mind to be a saint. I intend to keep out of all scrapes, and behave with perfect propriety all the time, night and day."

"I hope you are not jesting, Richard," said Bertha, who did not like the facetious language with which he clothed his resolutions.

"I'm in earnest. I mean every word I say. I solemnly promise you that I will be a pattern of propriety; but I don't like the Tunbrook Military Institute. I don't like the idea of being tied down to Colonel Brockridge's little finger; of being drummed and fifed here and there; and of reciting a Latin lesson at six o'clock in the morning, after an hour's drill on the parade ground. Berty, to tell you the truth, I don't believe I shall be able to keep my good resolutions, if I am to be tied to a bell rope, or have to move by the tap of a drum."

"I hope you will."

"If I could stay at home, and have my pony and my boat, I should do first rate."

Whatever the experienced reader may think of Richard's sincerity, he was uttering an honest opinion. He sincerely feared that his courage would not be equal to the work of submitting to the discipline of Tunbrook, and conquering himself, at one and the same time. Tunbrook and Colonel Brockridge seemed to be formidable obstacles in the path of reform.

"You would soon get used to the discipline of the Institute," suggested Bertha.

"I might get used to it as the old man's horse got used to living upon shavings — when he died. If I go, I shall try to submit; but I don't want to go."

"I don't see how it can be avoided. Father is determined that you shall go."

" You can save me from this strait jacket, if you will, Berty."

" What can I do, Richard ? "

" Mr. Presby will do any thing you ask him to do. You can tell him that you think it would injure me to be sent to Tunbrook. Then he can talk with father about it; and father will do any thing that Mr. Presby wishes."

Bertha promised to speak to Mr. Presby about the matter, and she did so at once ; but instead of Bertha convincing him that it would injure Richard to be sent to the Military School, he convinced her that it would be the best thing in the world for him.

" I am afraid I spoiled my own children by over indulgence, and I cannot counsel your father to do the same thing," said the old gentleman, with deep feeling.

Bertha returned to her brother with his answer. Richard was not angry, as she feared he would be, and this was a very hopeful sign. But he went over his argument against strait jackets, bell ropes, and drums and fifes, once more, and then proposed that he should be put on probation for one or two months ; and if he did any thing wrong, he would submit without a murmur.

Bertha went to Mr. Presby again, and was so far successful that the old gentleman agreed to speak with Mr. Grant in the evening. He kept his promise, but the father carried a stronger argument than the friend of the family. Richard was doomed to go to the Military Institute, and the fact was patent to him before he retired. He felt as though he wanted to submit, but the unconquered enemy that had so often led him astray was rebellious.

He did not sleep well that night. He was excited by the prospect before him. His good resolutions seemed to be very shaky, and he found himself running away from them. When he heard the clock strike twelve, he actually jumped out of bed, under a sudden impulse, fully resolved to run away and go to sea. He thought he would take the Greyhound, and make his way down to the city and ship the next day. He put on a portion of his clothes, under the influence of this impulse.

" This would be becoming a saint with a vengeance ! " said he to himself, as he threw off his
clothes, and got into bed again. " I told Bertha I
would try to submit, and I will."

This was the first decided advantage which Richard had gained over his great enemy; but the
battle was a mere skirmish with the outposts of
the potent foe. It was a victory, however, and it
strengthened him. It improved the *morale* of his
fighting element.

He had resisted temptation, and angels ministered unto him. While they ministered, peace came,
and he fell asleep.

At an early hour in the morning he was called
by his father. With the assistance of Bertha he
packed his trunk and prepared himself for the
journey. He was sad, but submissive. At nine
o clock, having bid adieu to all his friends, and
taken a sorrowful survey of Woodville, he and his
father were driven down to the railroad station.

Before night they reached Tunbrook, and Richard was introduced to the terrible Colonel Brockridge. He was a little man of fifty, with great

11

bushy red whiskers, whose whole face seemed to be eclipsed by the wonderful sharpness of his eyes. He shook hands with Richard, spoke to him very kindly, and hoped they should be good friends. The new recruit was shown to his quarters, as his room was called, and Mr. Grant took his leave.

Richard felt that he was alone with the future.

CHAPTER X.

RICHARD LEARNS THE MEANING OF RIGHT
ABOUT FACE.

THE apartment to which Richard was shown was called " Barrack B." There were ten rooms of this kind, known by the first ten letters of the alphabet, omitting J. Each barrack contained twenty narrow iron bedsteads, and no two boys were allowed to occupy the same bed. At the head of each barrack, there was an alcove large enough to contain the bed of the assistant teacher, who had charge of the pupils in the room. This apartment of the instructor was screened from the view of the boys by a curtain, so that he could see without being seen, when he desired to do so.

There was a small closet in the wall between every two beds, for the use of the boys, and Richard was directed to transfer the contents of his

trunk to this receptacle, by Mr. Gault, the assistant teacher in charge of Barrack B. Richard
opened the trunk, and then sat down upon the
bed to wait until the instructor should retire, for
he did not care to exhibit his wardrobe to a
stranger.

"Proceed, if you please," said Mr. Gault.

"I think I will do this business by myself,"
replied Richard.

"According to a rule of the Institute, the wardrobe of each pupil must be inspected," said the
teacher.

"Inspected?" asked the recruit. "What for?"

"To see that no improper articles are brought
in."

"I would rather not," added Richard.

"The rule is imperative," said Mr. Gault, decidedly.

The strait jacket had already begun to oppress
the male heir of Woodville, and he was disposed
to resent the indignity, as he deemed it; but almost the last words of Bertha had been an in-
junction to observe the rules of the school, how-

ever distasteful they might be. Reluctantly, and
with the feeling that he was sacrificing his inde-
pendence, Richard transferred his clothing to the
closet assigned to him. Mr. Gault carefully watched
the proceeding, and confiscated several articles which
were declared to be contraband, among which were
some cakes and other sweetmeats, prepared by
Bertha, and several yellow-covered novels he had
purchased in Whitestone.

" Can't I have those things ? " asked Richard.

" No, sir ; no boy belonging to the Institute is
allowed to eat cake on the premises."

" Why not ? "

" We do not explain to boys the reason for every thing we do," replied Mr. Gault, rather curtly.

" I don't think you have any right to take my
property away from me."

" I don't ask your opinion, and it is of no value
whatever."

" You needn't be so crusty about it," said
Richard, who was wholly unused to this style of
remark.

" We tolerate no impudence here. If you use an

11 *

expression of that kind again, you will be put under arrest, and spend the night in the guard house."

Richard's blood was beginning to boil, and he was tempted to pitch into the insolent instructor who dared to use language of that kind to the only son of the proprietor of Woodville. But he did not want to get into trouble the first day; besides, the words "arrest" and "guard house" had a very ominous sound to him.

"Can't I have my books? They are not cake," asked Richard.

"No, sir; you cannot. Such trash as that is not fit for boys to read. Your property will be kept safely for you, and when you leave the school, you can have it again."

"The cake will not be very good then."

"You can do any thing you please with it, except eat it. You can sell it, or give it away."

"You can do what you like with it."

"Very well. Have you any money about you?"

"I have."

"You will hand it to me, and a receipt for the amount will be forwarded to your father."

"Do you mean to rob me?" demanded Richard, his face flushing at this new indignity.

"I refer you to the regulations of the Institute. We provide every thing the boys require, and they have no more use for money than they have for wings."

"I won't give up my money."

"Very well, sir. I will refer the matter to Colonel Brockridge, and you may settle it with him. Follow me, if you please," said Mr. Gault, after Richard had locked the trunk containing the contraband articles.

The new scholar followed the teacher to the office of the principal on the first floor. He was very uneasy and nervous, and almost wished he had given up his money. But he felt that the tutor was carrying things altogether too far. It was subjecting him to a needless indignity.

"This young man refuses to give up his money," said Mr. Gault to the colonel, who was writing at his desk.

Without waiting to ascertain the result of the interview, the assistant departed, leaving the obdurate youth alone with the owner of those terribly sharp eyes.

"Have you read our regulations, Grant?" said Colonel Brockridge, turning round and looking the recruit full in the face.

But there was a pleasant smile upon his face, and his words were gentle, and even respectful.

"Yes, sir," replied Richard.

"Then you are aware that pupils are not allowed to have money — are you not?"

"Yes, sir."

"Boys are tempted to purchase various articles which injure them, such as cakes and candy, and improper books. Therefore we think it is better that they should not be provided with money. Is this a satisfactory explanation?"

"I don't know but it is, sir," replied Richard, doubtfully.

"It satisfies me, at any rate. How much money have you?"

"About five dollars."

"Now, Grant, if you will hand it to me, I will give you a receipt for it, or send it to your father.

I will keep it, subject to your order, if you desire it."

" I don't like the rule, sir."

" I think it is an excellent ·rule. But you waste
my time. Your decision, Grant."

" I should like to think of the matter, sir."

" Your decision at once," said the colonel; and
Richard saw the sharp eyes grow a shade sharper,
and heard the deep voice grow a shade sterner.

The recruit winced under the necessity thus laid
upon him. The principal could not be trifled with,
and he must either submit, or take the consequences, which were so indefinite to him that they
seemed sufficiently terrible.

" I will give up the money," said he, with a .
struggle, as he handed his wallet to the colonel.

" I am glad to find you are a discreet and sensible youth," added the colonel, as he wrote the
receipt, and handed it, with the wallet, from which
he had taken the money, back to the owner. "If
you wish to use money for any proper purpose,
you can draw on me, and your paper shall be
honored to the extent of the funds in my hands."

"I don't think I am likely to want money here," answered Richard, gloomily.

"Every needed article will be furnished. Now, Grant, I am afraid you have come here with an intention to resist our wholesome regulations. If so, you must learn the meaning of "right about, face" — in its moral application, I mean. Your father has told me all about you, and given me explicit instructions to make a man of you. I understand your case perfectly. If you are disposed to observe the rules of the Institute, we shall treat you like a gentleman. The future is before you, young man, and you must choose for yourself."

"I intend to obey the rules, sir," said Richard, rather crest-fallen after what had happened.

"I am very glad to hear you say so. In a few days you will be provided with the uniform worn by the pupils of the Institute. Here is a time card for the fall term. Look it over carefully, for you will be required to conform to it very strictly. To-morrow morning you will take your place with the boys, and go through with the programme just as though you had been here all your lifetime. We make no allowances for beginners; they will have seasonable warning, and they must be on the ground promptly at the moment. There will be a dress parade in a few moments, and you can go out and witness it, if you choose," said Colonel Brockridge, as he handed Richard the card. "After supper, Mr. Gault will introduce you to the boys of your barrack."

Richard took the card, and left the room. As he passed out of the building he descried the boys at play on the lawn. They were all dressed in a uniform of gray cloth, though some wore a loose blouse, and some, in the heat of play, had thrown off their jackets. The new scholar walked over to the flagstaff, where the stars and stripes were flying, and seated himself on a bench. The boys seemed to be having a good time, in spite of the strictness of the discipline. As he listened to the tremendous noise they made, and saw the rough-and-tumble games in which they were engaged, he became convinced that the Institute was not of the Blember style, and he began to have some hope that he should survive the shock.

While he was waiting for the dress parade, he examined the time card given him by the principal. To him it had a decidedly strait-jacket odor, and he read it with a feeling of repugnance, not to say disgust. It was as follows: —

"TUNBROOK MILITARY INSTITUTE.

FALL TERM.

From Sept. 1 *to Dec.* 1.

6	A. M.	Reveille.
6.30	"	Study.
7.30	"	Breakfast.
8	"	Squad Drill.
9	"	Study and Recitation.
11	"	Battalion Drill.
1	P. M.	Dinner.
1.30	"	Recreation.
3	"	Study and Recitation.
5	"	Recreation.
6	"	Dress Parade.
6.30	"	Supper.
7	"	Off Time.
9	"	Retire.

☞ The 'Off Time' belongs to the student; but deficient lessons must be made up during these hours.

☞ Camp duty will be performed by all students for one week, in each term, except the winter term.

J. BROCKRIDGE,

PRINCIPAL."

Richard thought the time card was rather formidable, but he came to the conclusion that he could stand it, if the rest of the boys could.

While he was musing upon the present and the future, the rattling drum sounded, and the boys instantly suspended their play. In a moment the whole crowd had disappeared within the buildings that flanked the lawn; but presently the rattle of several drums was heard, and one company after another marched upon the parade ground, and formed the line. Every boy was dressed in full uniform now, the blouses and other non-conforming garments having been thrown aside, and every one wore white gloves.

Richard found that the teachers were not the

officers of the companies, or the battalion, as he had expected. Several of the instructors were present, but they appeared to take no part in the proceedings. Every thing was managed by the boys, apparently without any assistance from the teachers The captains, lieutenants, sergeants, and corporals were all in appropriate uniform, with their rank designated as in the United States army. The swords and muskets were genuine weapons, though not so large and heavy as those used by older soldiers. The students varied in age from fourteen to eighteen.

The various evolutions of the dress parade were regularly performed. The adjutant announced to the major that the parade was formed; the band, consisting of eight pieces, marched up and down the line; the first sergeants reported "all present or accounted for," and the company officers marched up to the commander of the battalion. The boys were as rigid as statues when the order, " Parade —rest," was given. The companies marched back to the armories, broke ranks, and were dismissed.

Richard was delighted with this exhibition, and

the Tunbrook Military Institute went up many degrees in his estimation. He followed the boys into the supper room, where, without much ceremony, he made the acquaintance of several captains and lieutenants. He received a hearty welcome from his new associates, and began to feel very much at home.

The supper was not exactly what he had been accustomed to at Woodville, but it was plain wholesome food; and when he saw officers and privates, from the major down to the drummers, partake of it with hearty relish, he was not disposed to grumble.

After supper, the boys scattered in every direction. Some went out doors, some to the barracks, some to the school rooms. It was "off-time," and without much assistance from Mr. Gault, who attempted to introduce him, he made the acquaintance of half the students in the Institute. At nine o'clock the sound of the drum rolled through the halls, and the boys all retired.

CHAPTER XI.

RICHARD GOES THROUGH THE DRILL, AND HAS
A SET-TO IN THE GROVE.

RICHARD slept very well, and was attending to the business of sleeping with great pertinacity, when the reveille sounded at six o'clock in the morning. He did not feel much like getting up, and though the other boys in Barrack B instantly jumped out of bed, he did not heed the summons. It went against his grain to get up at the sound of a drum, or of a bell; not that he cared to lie in bed any longer, but the principle of the thing was utterly objectionable.

"Come, Grant," said the boy who occupied one of the beds next to him, in a kind and friendly tone, "it's time to turn out."

"I suppose it is," yawned Richard, "but I'm not quite ready to get up yet."

" Better get up at once. They call the roll to
half past six. You are in our company, you know."

" Suppose I don't get up—what then?"

" It will be all the worse for you."

" What will they do?"

" I don't know; but fellows don't like to be
late at roll-call."

Richard concluded to get up, for he preferred to
see a punishment inflicted upon some one besides
himself before he got into trouble. Bailey—for this
was the name of the boy next to him—told him
what to do, and where to go, till they made their
appearance at the armory of Company D, to which
the recruit had been assigned. They were then
sent to the school room for an hour's study.
Richard was examined to ascertain his attainments,
and placed in a class, and he was told to prepare
himself for the lessons of the day. There was no
great hardship in this, and as Richard's talents
were of a high order, he had no difficulty in per-
forming the work assigned to him.

The breakfast call scattered the boys again, and
they were soon reassembled in the dining room.

When they were seated, profound silence reigned throughout the apartment. The principal, all the assistant teachers, and every one else belonging to the establishment, were present. The chaplain then read a short passage from the Scriptures, which was followed by a prayer, the whole service occupying not more than three or four minutes.

The breakfast consisted of coffee, beefsteak, potatoes, with cold bread and butter. The new comer was perfectly satisfied with this fare, and taking it as a sample of his living, he did not believe he should starve.

"What next, Nevers?" asked Richard of the boy who sat next to him, and who wore the designation of an orderly sergeant.

"Squad drill, my boy. We shall give you some now," replied Nevers. "We begin to find out what a fellow is made of on drill."

There was a little spare time before the drill came on, and the new student improved it by inquiring particularly into the nature of his duties. Bailey was patient and communicative, and he obtained from him all the information he wanted.

Again the drum rattled, and the boys made their way to the several armories. The doors and windows were thrown open, and the drill commenced. It was conducted by Mr. Gault, who was assisted by various officers of the company.

"Nevers," said the assistant, "you may take Grant and instruct him in the positions."

Richard glanced at the orderly sergeant to whom this command had been given, and the look of satisfaction which Nevers put on did not please him.

"This way, if you please, Grant," said the young orderly sergeant, as he led the way to one corner of the armory.

"What are *you* going to do?" demanded the recruit.

"Give you the positions."

"Are you my teacher?"

"I am ordered to give you the positions," replied Nevers, chuckling with a delight which the new comer could not understand.

"You want to find out what I am made of — don't you?" said Richard, remembering what the other had said to him at breakfast.

" I always obey orders."

" Well, I think I should rather be instructed by
the regular teachers."

" Very well ; I will report to Mr. Gault."

" You needn't trouble yourself. If this is the
custom, go ahead. I am ready."

" Stand as I do, if you please — heels on
the same line, feet turned out equally, knees
straight."

Richard observed all these instructions, and being
a very tractable scholar, he was soon master of the
positions.

" Eyes — right ! " continued Nevers, explaining
the meaning of the order. " Front."

There were three other boys, who had not yet
been supplied with uniforms, having come to the
Institute a few days before. These also were
placed in Nevers's care, and he began to drill
them in the facings.

" Attention — squad," said the drill master, explaining what he meant, and going through with the
next movement. " Right — face."

Richard did not come to time, and the sergeant

repeated his instructions, and gave the order again; but it was done no better than the first time.

" Move quicker, Grant. How long will it take you to turn on your left heel? Now, try again. Right — face ! "

The young gentleman from Woodville did not like the style of the drill master's remarks. Though he had been scrupulously polite in all he had said, up to the point of Richard's failure to obey the order with promptness, there was something in his tone and manner that was very offensive to him. Nevers seemed to feel that he was armed with authority, and he intended to make the new comer feel it; but Richard took his own time, and after they had tried half a dozen times, he could not " right face " till after the others had completed the movement.

" How long will it take you to turn on your heel, Grant ? " said Nevers, sharply, when his patience had been sorely tried.

" Till you speak a little more civilly," replied Richard, quietly. " Perhaps not till you have found out what I am made of."

Nevers bit his lip at this reply. Perhaps he was conscious that he ought not to have used the remark, or he might have reported the contumacy of the recruit to the assistant in charge of the room.

"We will try again," continued Nevers. "Right — face."

The result was no better than before; for Richard was so offended at the manner of the instructor that he determined not to obey.

"Well, Grant, you won't get round till the first day of January. You are a perfect dough-head," said Nevers, the last remark being in a low tone, though it was distinctly heard by the subject of it.

"All right," muttered Richard. "If you have found out what my head is made of, I will show you, by and by, what my fist is made of."

"Ready when you are," replied Nevers, dropping his voice so that the assistant teacher could not hear him. "Now, about — face;" and he explained the movement, and went through with it himself.

Richard, having made up his mind what to do

when the occasion offered, did not deem it necessary to carry his resistance any farther at present
Besides, he was very desirous of learning the drill,
that he might join the company.. His " about face,"
therefore, was unexceptionable.

" Very well, Grant," said the drill master, in a
satirical tone, and with a patronizing air.

" Your praise and your censure are all the same
to me. Spare me both, if you please," replied
Richard, with a dignity becoming the male heir
of Woodville.

" No impudence, you puppy !" growled Nevers,
his check flushed with anger. " If Gault wasn't
here, I'd boot you."

" I will make an opportunity for you when he
is not present. Do your duty like a decent fellow, if you can," answered Richard.

" Squad, forward — march," said Nevers, as he
explained how the command was to be executed.

As Richard and his companions in the squad
were very tractable scholars, they soon mastered all
the mysteries of the step in common time, and were
then instructed in the principles of the " double

quick." They were then reviewed several times in
what they had learned; after which muskets were
placed in their hands, and they were taught to
"shoulder arms," "support arms," and "present
arms."

The hour devoted to drill was finished, and in
spite of the overbearing manner of the instructor,
Richard was pleased with the exercise, and even
began to entertain visions of military glory.

The two hours devoted to study and recitations
passed off without any thing to distinguish them.
Richard had learned his lessons, and every thing
went off to his satisfaction. The next item on the
time card was the battalion drill. The recruits
were placed in the ranks, and for an hour and a
half they were exercised in the school of the battalion; part of the time by Colonel Brockridge,
and part of the time by the young gentleman who
had been elected by the company officers to the
command of the battalion — Major Morgan. If
Richard was pleased with the squad and company
drill, he was delighted with that of the battalion.

After 'dinner came the hour of recreation. During this time the boys were allowed to go any where upon the estate, which contained about a hundred acres of land. Some of them made up games on the parade ground, and others went over to the grove, a short distance from the Institute buildings. Richard and Bailey, who had become good friends in the short time they had been acquainted, took a walk over the estate. They found the students engaged in every amusement which the genius of a boy could devise, from base ball and cricket down to mud dams and water wheels.

In the grove they found Nevers, whom Richard was very anxious to meet. The orderly sergeant was a year older than Richard, and somewhat heavier.

"There is the fellow I've been looking for," said Richard to his companion.

"Who — Nevers?"

"Yes, that's his name."

"Do you know him?"

"He drilled our squad this morning, and took the trouble to insult me several times."

13

" Just like him.   He is the biggest bully in the school."

" I am going to knock some of his impudence out of him."

" You ? " exclaimed Bailey, stopping short, and looking with astonishment at the new comer.

" I am going to try it, at any rate," added Richard, more modestly.   " I don't let any fellow insult me."

" Why, he will break every bone in your body. He can lick any fellow in the school."

" I don't care for that.   I won't be imposed upon by him."

" But it won't do ; if any fellow gets up a fight here, it goes hard with him."

" Can't help that."

" But he will whip you, as sure as you attempt it.   I tell you he is the bully of the school."

" He called me a dough-head, on drill, this morning."

" If you had reported him to Mr. Gault, he would have punished him severely.   No officer is allowed to speak impudently to a private, especially to a new fellow. Why didn't you report him?"

"Because I feel able to fight my own battles; besides, I don't like the idea of being a telltale."

"I advise you not to touch him. He will make mince meat of you, if you do."

"Perhaps he will; he shall have a chance to try it."

"I should like to see him licked, and so would every other fellow in the school."

"I think I can take care of him."

"Do you know any thing about the science?"

"O, well, something," replied Richard, with assumed indifference.

But Richard had been very thoroughly educated in the science of self-defence by Bob Bleeker, who had served his time as a butcher's boy in New York city, and done duty there as a rough of the first water.

"Nevers knows all about it. He has had half a dozen pitched battles with fellows whom he bullied, and all of them got whipped. Nevers has been 'cock of the walk for the last year, for no fellow dares say a word to him."

Richard said no more, but went directly to the place where the bully was standing. He walked up to him with a bold and defiant air.

"I am glad to meet you, Nevers," said he, with easy self-possession.

"Are you, my fighting chicken?" laughed Nevers.

"You called me a dough-head this morning," added Richard.

"I did; and to make sure that there is no mistake, I repeat it — You are a dough-head."

"Then take that for your impudence!" said Richard, as with a sudden movement he slapped the bully's face.

"A fight! A fight!" shouted the dozen boys who were gathered in that part of the grove.

"What do you want, Grant?" demanded Nevers, turning pale and red with rage. "Do you want me to lick you?"

"If you please. You wanted to know what I am made of. I am ready to show you."

" Clear the ring!" shouted the boys, forming a circle round the two belligerents.

Richard coolly threw off his jacket and vest rolled up his shirt sleeves, unloosed his suspenders, and wound them round his waist, to support his pants. Nevers threw off his jacket only. By this time, at least fifty boys had assembled to witness the encounter; and so unpopular was the bully, that Richard had the sympathy of the whole crowd, except a few personal friends of his opponent.

" I am all ready," said Richard, taking the most approved attitude.

" So am I," replied the ready Nevers, as he edged up to Richard, and attempted to plant a blow by the side of his head, which was handsomely parried, and a left-handed rap lodged under the eye of the bully.

This blow maddened Nevers, and he redoubled his efforts to crush his opponent, as he had expected to do at the first onset. " Keep cool, and have both eyes open," had been the oft-repeated admonition of Richard's distinguished instructor in the sublime art of self-defence, and he carefully observed the instruction. After a few more plunges on the part of Nevers, he found himself on the ground, from the effect of a stunning blow which Richard had given him on the side of the head.

" Are you satisfied ?" called Richard, flushed with victory.

" No ! " yelled Nevers, as he sprang to his feet, and rushed upon his antagonist.

Richard's coolness enabled him to do wonders, and the bully was down again in a moment more.

" Come on if you are not satisfied," said Richard, whose nose was bleeding, and on whose face there was a huge swelling, caused by the bully's hard fist.

" Time ! " shouted the boys.

" Gault's coming ! Dry up ! " " Settle it another time," added others, as they began to scatter.

CHAPTER XII.

RICHARD DOES A " BIG THING," AND TAKES THE CONSEQUENCES.

IN the language of the " prize ring," Nevers was still able to " come to time ; " therefore Richard could not be regarded as the victor in the fierce contest. The boys who formed the ring began to scatter as soon as the coming of the assistant teacher was announced. But they helped the combatants to clothe themselves, and used every effort in their power to conceal the fact that a fight had taken place.

" A drawn battle," said one of the students.

" Grant," said Nevers, " I am far from being satisfied. At five o'clock, if you are ready, we will finish this business."

" With all my heart," replied Richard, wiping the blood from his nose.

"I hope you will do so," said the bully, earnestly.

"You hope I will! Do you suppose I will not? I am willing to be put under bonds to appear at the time named, Nevers. If any body backs out, I shall not be the one."

"I am sure I shall not."

"Good!" shouted the boys.

"Now, keep still, fellows," added Nevers. "Don't say a word about it, or all the fun will be spoiled."

The spectators of the barbarous spectacle all promised to keep still, and Richard moved over to a brook behind the grove to wash the blood from his face. His opponent had sundry very bad-looking places on his physiognomy, but no blood had been drawn.

By this time Mr. Gault made his appearance in the grove; but so well did the boys play their parts, that he did not even suspect that any unusual event had transpired. Some of them commenced a game of "tag," and played with such zeal that no one could have suspected they

were not in earnest. Others engaged in conversation, and those who had followed Richard to the
brook resumed their labors upon the dam and
water wheel.

Mr. Gault had no particular motive in visiting
the grove. He was merely taking a walk in the
discharge of his duty, which included a general
supervision of the boys on all the grounds. But
Richard kept out of his way, fearful lest his
swelled face should betray him, and thus prevent
the final settlement of the account. He felt like
a victor already, for he was perfectly confident
that his superior science and coolness would give
him the battle.

I am sorry to add that he did not think of
the good resolutions he had made; or, if he did,
he banished the thought as inconvenient and uncomfortable. He really believed that he had been
deeply injured by the bully of the Institute, and
if he did not regard it as a positive duty to
obtain satisfaction, he at least felt that such a
course was perfectly justifiable.

Nevers was the bully of the school. Weak

and timid boys were obliged to submit to his insults. He had won the position of the "best man" in the school, and he employed his power in playing the tyrant. Richard felt that he must either whip him, or acknowledge him as his superior, and submit to his rule.

The element of pride also had a powerful influence upon his mind. Bailey had told him that Nevers could whip any fellow in the Institute; and it followed, of course, if he could master him, he should at once become the champion of the ring. Richard regarded this as a proud distinction, and he was quite willing to have a battered nose and a swelled face in the achievement of such an honor.

More than all this, Richard was animated by the generous sentiment that, in fighting and whipping the bully of the ring,'he became the champion of the weak and the timid, who dared not resent the insolence of Nevers.

When he had washed his face and stopped the bleeding, he followed the course of the brook, till t emptied itself int the river, which was a small stream some four or five rods wide. He was attended by Bailey and two or three other boys, who had suddenly conceived a very great admiration for him. If he was not the victor in the fight, he had the advantage, and he had already partially entered upon the enjoyment of the honors which would be bestowed upon the conqueror of Nevers.

A short distance above the mouth of the brook, the river received the waters of the beautiful and picturesque Tunbrook Lake. The Institute grounds bordered upon it for some distance, and great was the satisfaction of Richard when he saw several boats, which his companions informed him belonged to the school. There was a large schooner-rigged sail boat, two twelve-oar race boats, besides three smaller craft. He felt at home here, and inquired particularly whether the boys were allowed to use these boats. They were only permitted to sail in company with some of the instructors.

The boys were exercised in rowing on Saturday afternoons, when the regular sessions of the school were suspended, and also upon the occasional holidays which were granted. The lake was seven miles long, by about two in breadth, so that there was abundant sea room. While they were examining the boats, and viewing the beautiful lake, the signal bell in the tower of the Institute school room sounded its warning peal, and summoned them to study and recitation.

" How does my face look, Bailey ? "

" Not very bad."

" Do you think Gault will smell a mice when he hears my lessons ? "

" I don't see why he should."

" I guess I can stave him off if he does," added Richard, confidently. " Didn't you see me tumble down when that fellow chased me ? "

" What fellow ? " asked Bailey.

" Any fellow you please," replied Richard, with a knowing smile.

" I didn't see any fellow chase you," added Bailey, innocently.

" Can't you see through a millstone when there is a hole in it ? "

" Of course I can."

" Don't you see what I mean ? "

" No, I don't."

" If Gault asks me how I hurt my face, I will tell him a fellow was chasing me, and I tumbled down. Of course all the rest of you saw it."

" But I don't see it," persisted Bailey.

" Don't you, indeed ! Then I think you ought to have a pair of leather spectacles."

" O, I know what you mean, but I don't believe in lying about it."

" Ah, then you are a military saint — are you ? " said Richard, with a sneer.

" All but the saint," laughed Bailey. " I don't think there is any use in lying about it."

" Then I suppose you think it was very wicked of me to fight with Nevers."

" No, I don't," answered Bailey, promptly and decidedly. " Nevers is a bully, and he insulted you. My father always told me never to take an insult, but he would thrash me for telling a lie."

" Well, Bailey, I believe you are right. I think it is mean to tell a lie; but how shall I manage it ? "

14

"Face the music. A fellow who can stand such a pounding as you have had, wouldn't mind being punished."

" I don't like to be punished."

" I don't know as the colonel would punish you. If a fellow gets up a fight, he has to take it; but if he only defends himself, he says he does no more than his duty."

" Well, who got up this fight?"

" That's the point. Nevers insulted you, and you pitched into him. I don't know which is most to blame."

" We will leave it to the powers that be, and not bother our heads about the question I won't lie about it, any how."

By the time this point was settled the boys had reached the school room. Richard applied himself with zeal and patience to the labors of the afternoon, determined to do his whole duty. When called out to recite, Mr. Gault noticed the swelling upon his face, and at recess asked him what had caused it.

"It was done in a little affair out in the grove sir," replied Richard.

"What kind of an affair?"

"Nevers and I had a little set-to," said Richard

"Rather rough play, I should think," added Mr. Gault, as he struck the bell for the work to be resumed.

Richard congratulated himself that he had escaped, and, as he thought, without telling a lie. He told none with his lips, but his manner was such as to assure the teacher that the affair in the grove had been nothing but friendly sport. Deception, or wilfully misleading another, for the accomplishment of a purpose, is, in our opinion, just as culpable a falsehood as gaining the same end by a lie expressed in words. But Richard had not come up to this standard.

At the close of the school session, Richard hastened to the grove, as did all the boys who were in the secret of the fight. Nevers was on the ground soon after him, and the arrangements for the fight were hastily completed. A line of scouts reaching from the parade ground to the grove was

stationed at convenient distances to give warning
of the approach of any of the teachers. The ring
was formed, and Richard coolly divested himself of
all superfluous clothing, and prepared with the utmost care for the desperate encounter.

Nevers was ready sooner than Richard, for he
was not so precise in the arrangement of his garments. As he took his place in the ring, though
he stood strong and defiant, there was a kind of
nervousness in his manner, which might have been
detected by a keen observer.

" Come, Grant, we shall not get to work to-day,
if you don't hurry up," said Nevers, his lip curl-
ing into a sneer.

But it was the bully in him that spoke. He
had a reputation to sustain, and he was saying
and doing all he could to ward off any imputation
upon his courage.

" In one moment, Nevers," added Richard.

" You are as particular as though you were
going to a ball," continued Nevers.

" I suppose you are too much of a man to

bawl, whatever happens; so here won't be any,"
replied Richard.

- " We shall have the colonel and all the teachers
down upon us, if you don't get fixed soon."

" I'm all ready," said Richard, throwing himself
into the attitude of the pugilist.

" Come on, then."

Richard edged up to his antagonist, and after
considerable sparring, the fight commenced in good
earnest. Nevers was too much excited to use all
his strength to the best advantage, for the first
hit he received seemed to make him angry. In
the first round Richard had the advantage. In the
second, Nevers knocked him down; but he was not
at all disconcerted. The heavy blows he received
did not appear to disturb his equanimity, while his
opponent worked himself up into a towering passion. The fight went on for ten minutes with vary-
ing results. At one time all the spectators were
sure that Nevers would win, and at another they
were equally sure that Grant would be the victor.

The anger of Nevers exhausted him more than
his tremendous efforts. Both parties had been ter-

14 *

ribly punished, but Richard was still cool and self-possessed. At last Nevers became desperate, and rushed upon his foe, determined at one effort to crush him. He was furious, and abandoned all the science he had brought to his aid, and appar ently depended entirely upon brute force. The consequence was, that he laid himself open to his cool rival, and Richard rained a series of tremendous blows upon his head, which carried him under. He fell heavily upon the ground, and lay there incapable of moving.

Richard, though his nose was bleeding, and he could not see out of one eye, seated himself on the ground for a moment, till he had recovered his breath, and then took his place in the ring.

"Time!" cried the friends of Richard.

But Nevers could not "come to time." He raised himself partly up, but sank back again, incapable of making the effort to rise.

"Come on!" said Richard, as he sparred a little with his fists to assure the spectators that he was "game" to the last.

Nevers made no reply, and Richard was declared

the victor by his own friends, and the proposition was admitted by those of his prostrate antagonist.

"I am satisfied," added Richard, as he picked up his clothes, and made his way down to the brook, attended by an admiring crowd.

When Nevers recovered his breath, he rose from the ground, and his companions helped him down to the water, where he was bathed by his sympathizing friends. Both of the combatants were severely though not seriously injured.

"What's to be done now, fellows?" asked Richard, when all that cold water could do for him had been done. "I suppose we are all in a bad scrape."

"That's so," replied several. "We will stand by you, Grant, as well as we can."

"I am not exactly in condition to appear at dress parade," added Richard, turning his head round, so as to bring his available eye to bear upon his companions.

"You are better off than Nevers, who is first sergeant of Company D."

" Can't we keep out of sight till we get our
eyes open, as little kittens do ? "

" Roll call before dress parade," suggested Bailey.

" Can't some fellow answer for me? I will
spend the night in the cabin of the sail boat on
the lake. It won't be the first time I've slept in
a boat."

" That won't do. Better face the music, Grant."

" But I shall be punished for this affair. I
don't — "

" Colonel Brockridge is coming ! " was the word
passed down the line of scouts, interrupting Richard's remarks on the subject of punishment.

" What shall I do ? "

" Don't do any thing, Grant," said Bailey. " You
are sure to be found out, whatever you do. If
you run away, it will be all the worse for you."

Richard, after a moment's reflection, was of the
same opinion, and he decided to take the consequences, whatever they might be.

" What does all this mean ? " demanded the

colonel, sternly, when he saw the swelled face of Richard.

"Been a fight, sir," replied several of the boys

"Between whom?"

"Nevers and Grant."

"Nevers and Grant will report forthwith in my office," said the principal, as he walked back to the Institute.

CHAPTER XIII.

RICHARD LISTENS TO A HOMILY ON FIGHTING, AND SPENDS THE NIGHT IN THE GUARD HOUSE.

RICHARD, in obedience to the order of the principal, immediately repaired to the office, where he was soon joined by Nevers, both of them very much the worse for the encounter.

"You have been fighting — have you, young gentlemen?" demanded Colonel Brockridge, as he entered the room.

"Yes, sir," replied both of the culprits, in the same breath.

"You know the rules of the Institute, Nevers," added the principal, sternly.

"I do, sir; but I was struck, and was obliged to fight in self-defence."

"And you, Grant, had common sense enough to know better than to engage in a fight. You struck the first blow — did you?"

"I struck the first blow that was given with the fist, but Nevers struck the heaviest blow with his tongue."

"Explain, Grant."

"At breakfast I was informed by Nevers that they found out what boys were made of on drill."

"Did you make use of this remark, Nevers?" asked the principal.

"I did, sir."

"What did you mean by it?"

"Simply that we found out something about a boy's capacity."

"Ah, indeed!" added Colonel Brockridge, in a slightly satirical tone. "What did you understand by the remark, Grant?"

"That a fellow who hadn't spunk enough to protect himself must submit to be insulted, and to be bullied by those who were wiser than he in military matters."

"I did not mean that, sir," protested Nevers.

"His looks and his tone indicated it," said Richard. "And when he was directed to instruct me in the positions, his tone and manner were

haughty and domineering. I so understood it, sir;
if I am wrong, I am willing to apologize. In the
course of the drill he called me a dough-head."

"Is this true, Nevers?"

"It is; but I did not call him so till I was sat-
sfied he did not mean to observe the order. In
teaching him the facings, he would not come about
till all the others had finished the movement."

"I wouldn't, if I had been in his place," added
the colonel, very much to the astonishment of Richard, and very much to the indignation of Nevers.
"You know very well that one boy is never permitted in this school to domineer over another.
You took pains beforehand to inform Grant, by
your words, and especially by your looks and actions, that you meant to haze him, to bully him.
As a decent boy, he could not submit to it. Then
you called him a dough-head; which, as Grant
suggests, was the heaviest blow that was struck,
for it touches a spot which the fist cannot reach
Nevers, you commenced the fight."

"I think not, sir."

"We don't argue the matter, sir," said the

colonel, sharply. "One thing more: no pupil is allowed to use ungentlemanly language to another pupil. Obedience to officers who are merely students is purely voluntary. If a boy refuses to obey the officers, he must leave the company. No boy is compelled to go into the ranks. On drill the case is still stronger, Nevers. If the recruit will not obey, it is the duty of the drill officer to report him to the instructor. If you had done so, it would have been Mr. Gault's duty to drill Grant himself."

Nevers made no reply to these remarks. He cast a savage glance at Richard, who appeared to have conquered him in the forum as well as in the field.

"Grant, you are also to blame," continued the principal. "We will not permit you to be insulted, bullied, or domineered over. I will protect you, but you must not take the law into your own hands. A blow is not justifiable except in self-defence, or when all other means have failed. You knew it was wrong to strike Nevers."

"I did not think so, at the time, sir," replied

Richard. " What you have said has changed my
view of the matter."

Nevers sneered at this remark of his antagonist,
and Richard saw and felt that' sneer. It was as
much as to say that he, Richard, was making his
peace with the principal by pretending a penitence
he did not feel. It stung him where he was very
sensitive, and he was angry.

While his wrath was boiling, and he was considering in what manner he should punish his crest-
fallen rival for his savage look and his bitter sneer,
the parting admonition of Bertha came to his mind,
with the promise that he had made to obey the
rules of the school. This suggested his big resolutions to reform his life and character. A brutal
fight on the first day of his residence at Tunbrook
was not exactly redeeming his solemn promise to
his sister ; nor was the conquest of Nevers a step
towards the conquest of himself.

Yet, in spite of his promise, and in spite of his
resolutions, he could not believe that he had been
altogether in the wrong. He thought Colonel
Brockridge's views of the case were very sensible :

and while he wished he had not been so hasty in
hitting Nevers, he felt, as the principal had suggested, that his conduct was greatly palliated by
the provocation he had received.

Nevers cast looks of hatred and contempt at
him, which stirred his blood deeper than even the
words of insults he had received. He came to the
conclusion that the bully had not got enough yet,
and impulsively he determined to give him some
more at the first convenient opportunity. But when
he thought of the promise he had made to Bertha,
when he thought of his resolution to conquer himself, he struggled with the temptation, and finally
had the strength to say to the malignant demon
of hatred and revenge, " Get thee behind me,
Satan." The victory was won; the heart of Richard was at peace ; he had actually conquered himself this time.

" You have both done wrong," said the principal,
after a few moments' consideration, during which
time Richard had won a greater and nobler victory
than that he had gained in the grove.

" I am sorry for it," said Richard, and it was

almost the first time in his life that he had acknowledged himself in the wrong.

Nevers cast a look full of contempt at him
when he uttered these words; but Richard, under
the influence of the good angel which had taken
possession of his soul, did not permit the look to
ruffle him.

"I will do right, and feel right, this time, if I
never did before," said he to himself.

"Nevers," added the principal, "your warrant as
orderly sergeant is withdrawn; you are reduced to
the ranks. You can go, now. Remove those stripes
from your arms."

The sentence was a heavy blow to the bully.
For a year he had been trying to obtain promotion. He wanted a commission. The company
officers were elected from the sergeants, and he
was confident that he should be chosen captain
of Company D at the next election. He had
been a sergeant for a year and a half, and would
have been a captain if he had not been a bully;
for there were enough who disliked him on this
account to prevent his election. As the first

sergeant of the company, he was almost sure that he should be chosen the next time. But his sentence removed all hope of such preferment.

"Grant, I believe you are sincerely sorry for what has happened; but you have done wrong, and you must be punished."

Richard's anger rose at these words, and he was disposed to resent the idea of being punished for what he had done, especially after the judge had ruled so decidedly in his favor.

"I shall order you to be placed under arrest, and to spend the night in the guard house. You will report to me at dress parade. You can go."

The culprit's lips were compressed, and his teeth were tightly closed. He was angry, for he had expected to be fully justified before the boys for his conduct. An impudent remark trembled on the end of his tongue, but the memory of the conquest he had achieved over himself prevented him from uttering it.

"I have done wrong, and I have owned that I was in the wrong. I will submit," said Richard to himself, as he left the office.

15 *

When he went out upon the play ground, he found the boys assembled in groups discussing tho exciting event of the day. They gathered around him to learn the result of the trial.

"Nevers has lost his office, and I am under arrest, to spend the night in the guard house," replied Richard, in answer to their inquiries.   •

"You got off easy," said Bailey.

"I suppose I did; at any rate, I am satisfied."

"Nevers has lost his warrant," exclaimed the boys, who were particularly technical in speaking of military events. "Let's give three cheers."

"Don't do it," said Richard. "It's a hard case for him."

"I am glad of it. The bully is down," added one."

"You licked him well," said another.

"I am sorry I did," replied Richard. "I didn't understand the matter so well then as I do now. Colonel Brockridge is a trump!"

If any of Richard's friends at Woodville had heard this remark, they would have been ready to canonize him at once, for it was so utterly at variance with his style, that his acquaintances would not have recognized it as coming from him. But Richard was engaged in the conquest of himself, and had won two or three important victories.

The early call for dress parade sounded, and the boys all hasted to the armories to prepare for it. As Richard had no uniform yet, he was excused from serving, and reported himself to the colonel, as he had been ordered. When the parade was finished, the principal delivered a homily on fighting, stating the facts connected with the combat of that day, and commenting upon them. He condemned fighting in round terms, declaring it was never necessary, except in self-defence. The civil and the social law would protect every member of the community, and there could be no need of resorting to the barbarous custom of settling differences by single combat. He applied the principles he laid down to the case before him so clearly, that Richard lost much of his admiration of the "noble art of self-defence" — as pugilists stupidly style the act of fighting, to ascertain who is the better man.

Lest our boy friends should not fully understand us, we must add, that the colonel's views are ours. A boy ought to fight in self-defence; never to find out which is " the better man." He should use no more violence than is necessary to defend himself. A boy is bound to protect his weak friend — not from words, but from blows — to the best of his ability, by using blows, when they are necessary. We can excuse, but we cannot justify, the boy who strikes another for insulting his mother or his sister. We believe in a " kiss for a blow," but we also believe that cannon are often the best peacemakers. " Blessed are the peacemakers," but he who permits himself to be unjustly scourged is more truly a fomenter of strife than he who conquers a peace in a good cause by the might of his strong arm.

At the conclusion of his remarks, Colonel Brockridge ordered Richard to be conducted to the guard house, where he was to spend the night. Mr. Gault was directed to see the order executed, and the culprit was marched to the apartment which served as a place of confinement for offenders

Ho submitted to the punishment with the best grace he could command, but he was mortified and humiliated.

The guard house was a bugbear to the boys of the Institute. It was a small room, with the mockery of iron bars at the window, placed there more for effect than for any thing else. It contained a bed and a stool, with no other furniture. But it was regarded as a terrible place by the boys; not that it was a very great hardship to spend a night there, but because of the disgrace which the popular sentiment of the establishment had attached to the prison.

Richard entered, and the door was locked upon him. The room was dark, but he was not permitted to have a light. He seated himself upon the stool, and it was literally the stool of repentance to him. His supper was brought to him, and the servant stood by with a lamp till he had eaten it. He was then left alone for the night, to meditate upon the folly and wickedness of engaging in a fight without justifiable cause.

One of the first questions which the hero of the

fight asked himself was, whether he had not too
tamely submitted to the authority which had humiliated and punished him. That he had done so
was the most surprising thing he had ever known
himself to do. And when he came to ask himself
why he had submitted, he could very clearly trace
the reason to the good resolution he had made to
reform his life and character — to conquer himself.
It was hard for him to give in, but he was satisfied with himself, and began to feel that he had
really made some progress in the great work.

He wanted to write a letter to Bertha, and tell
her all about the events of the day — how patiently
he had submitted to reproof and punishment; and
record his solemn determination to conquer himself.
He had no light, and no materials for writing; so,
at an early hour, he went to bed; and fatigued
with the labors and excitement of the day, he forgot in sleep that he was a prisoner.

At reveille, in he morning, he was discharged
from arrest, and ordered to report for duty in the
school room. He was still strong in his good resolutions, and the sneers and frowns of Nevers and

his clique did not disturb him—did not even tempt him to indulge in the cheap retaliation of sneers and frowns in return.

In the course of the day Richard found that he was a lion. He had thrashed the bully of the school. and won the enviable position of champion of the Institute. But even this glory did not seem to be worth much ; for since the fight, he realized that he had whipped a bigger fellow than Nevers.

For a week, in school and out, Richard was true to himself, and behaved nobly. More times than we have room to record, during this period, he got the better of his ever-familiar foe, and every new victory improved his *morale* and added to his *prestige.*

At this point in his school career, the students were ordered to perform the usual round of camp duty ; and at eight o'clock in the morning, the battalion took up the line of march for the appointed place, at the other end of Tunbrook Lake, distant ten miles by the rail.

CHAPTER XIV.

RICHARD DOES GUARD DUTY, AND IS CAPTURED
BY AN ENEMY.

CAMPING out was a great event at Tunbrook, and the students looked forward to it with pleasant anticipations for weeks. The principal was shrewd in his policy, and no one knew when it would take place till it was announced, only a day or two before the march. By this plan he prevented any diversion of the thoughts from the lessons. Neither did the boys know where they were going when they started. They obeyed the orders which were given from time to time, and even when they halted for the night and pitched their tents, they could not find out whether they had reached the end of the march or not The colonel told them that soldiers should be taught to obey orders, and cured of all propensity to ask questions.

The tour of camp duty for the summer term had been almost a continuous march; and during the campaign of ten days, they had travelled over a hundred miles. Colonel Brockridge was an earnest believer in the necessity of physical development in boys. He was of the opinion that they could stand almost every thing, if they were regularly and systematically inured to hardship. Weak papas and tender mammas raised their hands with horror at the idea of having their Johnny sleep on the ground in a tent, and stick to the camp whether it was fair weather or foul; but the colonel could adduce hundreds of instances where boys of puny constitutions had become strong and vigorous under this treatment.

He believed that more boys had been spoiled by being "babied" than ever had been injured in the slightest degree by hardship — if military duty, as it was performed at Tunbrook, could be called hardship. It was very certain that the boys enjoyed camping out; and if a few of them sneezed or coughed after their return, these were not regarded as fatal symptoms.

16

Richard was in his element when the school was put upon its muscle. Though nothing but a private in Company D, and subject to the orders of his inferiors in body and mind, he performed his duty cheerfully, and enjoyed it very much. After Nevers had been cured of his folly, there was not another boy in the establishment who had the hardihood or the desire to impose upon him.

Every thing was done with military order and precision on the morning that the battalion marched from the Institute. Though the reader knows where they were going, not an officer or a private had a suspicion of their destination ; and none but a few of the new comers asked the question, or appeared to care. In front of the battalion was the band, and behind it came the wagons containing the tents, baggage, and pontoon train. The principal and the instructors were scattered along the line, where they could superintend the operations of the column.

Major Morgan, in command of the battalion, had evidently received instructions for a portion of the day ; for, without any direction from the teachers,

he led his command over the road to the grove,
and in fifteen minutes after they started, the order
to halt was given. The battalion stood rigid as a
stake where they were ordered, and presently the
engineer corps was detached for duty. The pontoon
wagon was brought up, and unloaded by the side
of the river. The boats, which were of rubber,
were inflated, and the business of building a bridge
across the stream was commenced.

  Every thing was so nicely prepared that the
work was accomplished in an incredibly short space
of time. The battalion, followed by its wagons,
crossed the pontoon bridge, the boats and the
planks were taken up and loaded upon the wagon
again, and the troops were ready to march. Neither
Colonel Brockridge nor any of the instructors had
spoken a word during these operations, for the
engineers had been thoroughly trained in their difficult duty.

  For an hour the battalion marched without stopping. The orders "shoulder arms," "support arms,"
"right shoulder shift" relieved them occasionally;
but some legs began to ache before a halt was

permitted. During the next hour they marched most of the way with the "route step." At twelve o'clock they halted for dinner and an hour's rest. The haversacks of the soldiers had been filled with crackers and cold ham, and they had a jolly dinner in a grove where they stopped.

About four o'clock in the afternoon, they reached the upper end of the lake, and the orders necessary for forming a camp were given. The tents were pitched, the boundaries of the camp marked out, and a detail for guard duty was made from each company. Every thing proceeded precisely as it would if they had been old soldiers, and engaged in the actual business of war.

Richard was one of those who had been detailed from Company D, for guard duty. The camp ground was a large, open plain, bordering on one side upon a dense forest. The night was dark and dismal, and at nine o'clock Richard found himself walking his lonely beat, on the verge of the forest. There was a novelty about the situation that was very attractive to him, and as he walked his solitary round, he actually enjoyed it. It was not to all probable that an enemy, or even a straggler, would disturb the quiet of the scene by attempting to pass the line ; but though the guard had been commanded to be vigilant, he had abundant time and opportunity for reflection and castle-building.

Our sentinel had imbibed much of the spirit of the soldier, from the martial exercise to which he had been trained, and he indulged in some pretty visions of military glory. They were very pleasant and very alluring at that time, when the country was enjoying profound peace. Even the politicians, who were compromising with difficulties, present and future, never dreamed that the war blast would sound through the land in their day and generation, and were unbelievers in the dire prophecies which they uttered. While Richard's fancy led him to scenes of blood and glory on the battle field, he little thought that an opportunity would so soon be presented for the practical application of his military knowledge, and for the indulgence of his military ambition.

While he was dreaming of war and glory, while in imagination he was leading battalions of brave

men to battle and victory, his reflections were disturbed by the approach of a squad of boys. It
was so dark that he did not see them till they
were within a few rods of him. It was evident
that they had left the tents by stealth, and must
have crept some portion of the way on the ground
to escape observation. When they came near
enough to be challenged, the guard called out, —

"Who comes there?"

"Friends," replied one of the party.

"Advance, one friend, and give the countersign."

One of them stepped forward, and Richard held
him at bay with his bayonet, according to military
custom.

"I declare, I have forgotten the countersign,"
said he.

"Then I will call the corporal of the guard."

"No; hold on a minute. I shall think of it in
a moment."

Richard was willing to give him a fair chance,
as there was no enemy in the vicinity who could
possibly intend to capture the battalion. But while
he was waiting, the fellow suddenly grasped his

musket, and attempted to wrest it from his hands. But this was a game at which two could play as well as one ; and Richard, instead of giving the alarm, as he should have done, threw himself upon his muscle, and attempted to beat off his assailants.

The rest of the party immediately came to the assistance of the fellow, and, after a short but sharp struggle,. the sentinel was overpowered, and his gun taken from him. At the conclusion of the struggle Richard found himself upon his back, on the ground, held down by the whole squad of boys, or as many as could get hold of him. One of them held a handkerchief over his mouth, so that he could not give the alarm, now that he found it necessary to do so.

Richard supposed this rough treatment could be nothing more than a practical joke — one of those tricks played off upon raw recruits, to teach them the necessity of vigilance, and a nice observance of the rules of the service. When he was overpowered, therefore, he submitted to his fate, whatever it might prove to be, hoping his captors would relax their hold upon him just long enough to enable him to turn the tables upon them; for he was vain enough to believe that he could whip the whole dozen of them, if he could only have fair play

"Let him up, now, and we will tie his hands behind him," said one of the party, in a feigned voice, to prevent the victim from recognizing the speaker.

"But he will halloo, if we let him up," replied the one who had answered his challenge, and whose voice Richard could not identify.

"I'll stop his mouth, if he hallooes," added the first speaker. "I'll hit him over the head with the butt of his musket."

"No, no," said the other; "you'll kill him. We don't want to injure him."

"I do; I wouldn't mind cracking his skull for him."

"No, no; we shall get into trouble ourselves if we do any thing of that kind."

Richard thought they would any way, as soon as he could obtain the use of his arms. He felt so well qualified to take care of himself that he would have been willing to give his bond not to halloo, or call any one to his assistance, though he could not help wondering that the sentinels whose beats were next to his own, did not arrive at the scene of operations. It was evident to him that they were asleep on their posts, or that they were accomplices of the conspirators.

" Now, get up," said the speaker, who used the disguised voice.

Richard promptly obeyed this order, and though several of the boys held on to him as he rose, a terrible struggle ensued, in which the captured sentinel almost made good his mental boast; but they were too many for him, and his hands were tied behind him with a knapsack strap, in spite of his best exertions to shake them off.

" I told you he would be a hard customer," said one, who had not before spoken.

" Shut up, you ninny! You'll blow the whole of us. No fellow is to speak but — you know whom," said he with the assumed voice.

Richard tried to obtain, in the thick darkness that shrouded them, some clew which would enable him to identify the ruffians; but he could not make out any thing peculiar in their form or motions to guide him, and he was equally at fault in regard to the voices. He stood quiet when he found that resistance was useless; but he determined to keep a sharp lookout for an opportunity to release himself from his mortifying situation.

" Now, you — "

" My name is Dobbin," added the false voice.

Richard did not remember any such name, though he had heard the roll called in all the companies, and he concluded that it was a " blind," to deceive him.

" Now, Dobbin, take him off, and we will settle the case in the woods."

" Lead the way, Kennedy, and we will follow; but be careful and not make a noise."

" Hush!" said Dobbin; " somebody is coming."

" Grand rounds!" added Kennedy. " Hurry him off as quick as you can. Stuff a handkerchief in his mouth; choke him if he attempts to cry out."

" But they will miss him," suggested Dobbin, " and then there will be a row and a search."

"Off with him! Off with him! We shall all get caught," whispered Kennedy. "I will take his gun, and keep guard."

Richard was literally dragged from the spot, and the fellow who called himself Kennedy—though that was not his name—took the musket of the defeated sentinel, and began to travel his beat as regularly as though he had been duly detailed.

"Who comes there?" demanded he, as the officer of the day, attended by a sergeant and two men, approached his beat.

"Grand rounds," replied the sergeant.

"Halt, grand rounds! Advance, sergeant, with the countersign."

The sergeant advanced to give the countersign, without discovering that he had been challenged by the wrong man.

"*Bennington*," said the sergeant, giving the word appointed for the night.

"Advance, rounds!" added Kennedy, as he placed himself in the proper position.

The officer of the day passed on with his attend· ants, and as soon as the ceremony had been repeated with the next sentinel, Kennedy threw the musket upon the ground, and followed his companions into the forest. Taking a road which led into the wood, he soon overtook the rest of the party.

Richard was very curious to find out what his captors intended to do with him; for he could not even yet believe that any thing more serious than a practical joke was intended. He was not conscious that he had an enemy in the battalion, with the exception of Nevers, who, though he had bestowed a great many sneers and looks of hatred upon him during the week that had elapsed since the fight, had betrayed no intention to seek revenge for his defeat in fair fight. He knew that Nevers hated him, but he could not believe that he would resort to such underhand measures as the conspirators had adopted.

"What are you going to do?" asked he, after Kennedy had joined them.

"Shut up! You will find out soon enough."

Richard tried to open a conversation with them, but they were too wary to talk, and no one spoke except Dobbin and Kennedy. They conducted their prisoner half a mile, as he judged, from the camp, when they halted, and fastened Richard to a tree, seating themselves upon logs and stumps. The captive waited impatiently for the proceed- ings to commence.

17

CHAPTER XV.

RICHARD FINDS HIMSELF IN THE HANDS OF THE REGULATORS.

"Come, fellows, we have no time to spare," said Kennedy, when the party were seated, and Richard fastened to the tree. "We must finish this business at once."

"We are all ready," replied Dobbin.

"Ready for what?" demanded Richard.

"Ready to settle your case. We are going to give you the biggest licking you ever had in your life."

The prisoner thought this was rather doubtful; but as they could not be supposed to have any knowledge of the thrashing inflicted upon him by "Old Batterbones," he was willing to excuse any exaggerations of which they might be guilty. When the young ruffian spoke of flogging him,

Richard could not help recalling the incident at the barn of the farmer on the Hudson. Then he was guilty, now he was innocent; and his feelings on the present occasion were as different from those of the former one as light is from darkness.

He had been captured while in the discharge of his duty, and was not conscious that he had given his assailants any cause of offence. He could not explain how it happened that he was not angry. He did not chafe in the bonds that confined him. The consciousness of being innocent of all offence before his comrades, sustained and supported him; and he felt a kind of proud superiority over his .captors, which placed him out of the reach of fear, and even out of the reach of malice and revenge.

Richard was a courageous boy; he had been so in his foolish and vicious enterprises; but he was doubly so now, when his soul was free from the stain of transgression. He did not borrow any trouble about what his persecutors intended to do, though he felt a very natural curiosity to see the end of the adventure.

"Go on," replied Richard, calmly, as the spokes-
man of the party anounced their intentions.

"Shall we tell him what for? Shall we try
him?" asked Kennedy.

"Yes; let us give him a drum-head court martial. The licking won't do him any good if he
don't know what it is for," replied Dobbin.

"Grant," said Kennedy, with the solemnity of
a judge, "you have ruined the best fellow in
Company D."

"He ruined himself," replied Richard.

"No, he didn't. Of what you did in fair fight in
the grove, we haven't a word to say. But you have
prejudiced the colonel against him, and caused him
to be deprived of his warrant, which will prevent
him from obtaining his commission at the next
election. You set yourself up as a leader among
the fellows before you had been a week in the
school. Have you any thing to say?"

"Nothing, except that all your charges are false,"
answered Richard; and if there had been light
enough to see it, a smile would have been discovered upon his countenance.

"In the interview with the principal, you pre-tended to be a saint, and to be sorry for what you had done. You did not stand up like a man, and take the consequences of your acts."

"Go on; I have nothing to say," added Richard, when the speaker paused.

"You are a dangerous fellow in the school. You intend to climb up yourself by pushing others down. We won't submit to it."

"What are you going to do?" coolly asked the prisoner.

"We are going to thrash you, as you deserve."

"You are brave fellows!" sneered Richard. "What you are afraid to do in the daylight, with fair play, you do by stealth and trickery in the night. You are a set of cowards, and if you will untie my hands I will whip the whole of you."

"That is very fine talk, Grant," said Kennedy, "but it don't amount to any thing."

"No talk is necessary to prove your cowardly meanness. Go on, and do your best. I am not afraid of the whole of you, even with my hands tied behind me. I despise the whole of you."

17 *

" We will give you a chance to escape."

" I don't ask any chance to escape."

" Grant, you talk like a fool."

" Better be a fool than a knave and a coward."

" We don't want to hurt you. There are fellows enough in our crowd to make Tunbrook Institute too hot to hold you. We advise you to
write to your father, advising him to send you to
some other school. Will you do so ? "

" I will not," replied Richard, promptly.

" Then you must take the consequences. We
are organized, and we are determined that you shall
leave. If you ask your father, and insist upon it,
no doubt he will take you away."

" Very likely he would," added Richard, " but I
shall not ask him to do so."

" You plainly don't understand what is in store
for you. Our plans are well laid, and we have
been through the same mill once before. A fellow
about your size, and one who could fight as well
as you do, had to leave about a year ago. He
undertook to be a leader before his time came.
We hunted him out, as we shall you."

" When you hunt me out, I will go, but not till then."

" Grant, this is all idle talk on your part. You don't understand your situation. We can count up fifty fellows belonging to our association. We can drive out any fellow who makes himself obnoxious. We mean to be fair, and we are willing that any fellow who works his way up should have all the honors he wins. But do you suppose we fellows, who have been here two or three years, and who have worked ourselves up, are going to step one side for a fellow who has been here only a week or two ?"

" Who asks you to step aside ?" demanded Richard, indignantly, for this show of fair play had touched him in a tender spot, and in spite of himself he began to be interested in the argument.

" You do; you have licked the best fellow in the school, and then you begin to play saint, and curry favor with the colonel. You mean to lead, and not follow."

" I mean to be and do just what circumstances require."

"Grant, there is no such thing as misunderstanding your position. What your looks indicate is more than all you may say with your mouth, or do with your hands. You are a dangerous fellow, and you must leave, or compromise."

"What do you mean by compromise?"

"We'll let you stay if you will keep in your proper position."

"What is my proper position?"

"At the foot of the ladder, of course, till the fellows above you have got out of the way."

"You mean Nevers?"

"Nevers and others."

"I will agree to no such compromise. All the officers, I am informed, are chosen by ballot."

"They are."

"Then, of course, the fellows can choose whom they please."

"They can; and since you have whipped Nevers, they will elect you; and those who have done their duty for two or three years must go into the shade. If you will agree to step one side, we will promise to let you alone. Will you do it?"

" I will not."

" Mind what you do, for if the ' Regulators' make war upon you, they will drive you out."

" The what ? "

" The Regulators. They are a secret society for certain purposes. It is a powerful organization, Grant, I can tell you. If you will do the right thing, we will take you in."

" No you won't. I'm not to be taken in by any such bait," replied Richard, who was disposed to laugh at the ridiculous association that had taken upon itself the duty of regulating the affairs of the Tunbrook Institute.

" You may sneer as much as you please. Every fellow in the school knows there is such a society, but no one but members can tell who belong to it. We mean to have fair play in this institution, and we have never yet failed in getting it."

" Come, Kennedy, you will talk all night," said Dobbin. " You can't do any thing with him."

" Well, Grant, you may leave, compromise, or take the consequences. Which will you do ? "

" I will not leave ; and I certainly will not compromise on the terms named. I mean to behave myself like a man, while I am here. If any one is a better fellow than I am, I will step one side for him, as I must. If any fellow gets above me in the class, I will not complain, or attempt to pull him down. If the fellows think I am fit to be a sergeant, or a captain, or a corporal, I shall abide their decision. I won't pull any fellow down, or be pulled down myself. I think the Regulators are a mean, dirty, cowardly set of bullies, who mean to build themselves up by pulling others down. Let every fellow be judged by his own merits. That's my opinion. Now you can do what you please."

And they did do what they pleased, though it was evident the Regulators were not accustomed to deal with so stubborn a subject. At the word from Kennedy, who seemed to be the chief of the society, the whole band fell upon Richard with sticks which they had cut in the woods, and gave him a most unmerciful beating. The prisoner bore it with silent disdain. He felt that the cause in

which he was engaged was a good one, and he
did not flinch from the penalty of fidelity.

At the word from the chief, they suspended the
flagellation, and Kennedy again attempted to bring
him to terms by argument, but it was in vain.

"Very well," said he, evidently disappointed at
the ill success of the reasoning process. "This is
only the first installment of what is your due.
When any thing goes wrong with you, when you
get into a scrape, when you find the ushers and
the colonel down upon you, just understand that
the Regulators are round. You have fifty enemies
now, instead of one, as you had two hours ago."

"That's all, Kennedy; don't say any more," interposed Dobbin, impatiently. "Let's take him
back now. He will find out the rest of it fast
enough."

If Richard could have heard the conversation
among the Regulators before they waited upon him,
he might have been flattered by the complimentary
manner in which his name was handled. His talents and his muscle, no less than his growing
popularity, were appreciated by the band, and it

was more desirable to win him than it was to drive him out. They knew what a valuable acquisition he would be to their number. But he must stand one side, and wait for his turn before he aspired to become a leader.

The Regulators, using the utmost caution, unloosed the prisoner, and marched him back to the camp. When they reached the line, they threw him upon the ground. While one of the largest of them, having all the advantage, held him there, the others disappeared in the darkness. The fellow that held him then removed the strap from the arms of the captive, and bounded away as fast as his legs would carry him.

Richard jumped up as quick as he could and gave chase. But the Regulator had the start of him, and the pursuit was useless. The victim returned to his beat, felt round upon the ground till he found his gun, picked it up, and resumed his solitary walk. He was a little confused by the events which had transpired, and he was forced to acknowledge that the Regulators had managed their business with consummate address and skill. He hardly knew what to make of the affair. He knew that he had been whipped; this fact was still patent to his consciousness in the tingling sensation that played over his legs.

The whole thing seemed very much like an illusion. It was almost too strange and ridiculous to be credited, and he could not help considering whether he had not actually been walking in his sleep this time. The Regulators appeared, to his sober senses, to be the most absurd institution ever invented by the mischievous brain of a boy. Yet he could not disbelieve the evidence of his senses, and especially of his smarting legs, and he was compelled to admit that the society actually existed; though there was a remote possibility that the whole affair was a practical joke, devised by Nevers and his clique.

We have before intimated, in the course of this story, that Richard Grant was an "old head." He had a very tolerable conception of the principles of strategy; therefore he did not do as most boys would have done — make a tremendous row over the occurrences of the night. He decided that it would

18

be politic for him to keep both eyes and both ears open, while he kept his mouth closed. By this course he hoped to obtain a clew to the mystery, and thus eventually to make the daylight shine in upon the dark proceedings of the Regulators.

"Where have you been this hour?" demanded the sentinel, whose beat was next to his own, when they met.

"I haven't been far off," replied Richard; "that is, not more than half a mile off," he added, in a tone so low that his companion could not hear him.

"I understand. You have been taking a nap."

"'Pon my word, I haven't."

"But you have; I haven't seen you before for an hour."

"I haven't been asleep."

"Honor bright, Grant, haven't you?" asked his companion, good naturedly.

"No, I haven't."

"Where were you when the grand rounds were made?"

"I was close by."

"Of course you were, or you would have been missed," added his neighbor, as he turned on his heel and made off.

Richard thought he was very easily satisfied, and he wondered if he wasn't a member of the secret band of Regulators. Our sentinel marched to the other end of his beat. His neighbor on this side had missed him, but he was as easily satisfied as the other had been, and Richard wondered whether *he* was not a Regulator.

While he was musing upon the extraordinary events of the night, the relief came round, and he was marched to the guard tent, where, for four hours, he had an opportunity to dream of the Regulators, and their secret management of the affairs of the Tunbrook Institute.

CHAPTER XVI.

RICHARD BECOMES FIRST SERGEANT OF COMPANY D.

THE next morning Richard was discharged from guard duty, and returned to the battalion. From the moment he opened his eyes he carefully observed the actions of his companions, and even studied the glances which were bestowed upon him. All his watching seemed to be in vain, for he could not obtain a particle of information that would aid him in solving the mystery of the Regulators.

Among the boys there were several with whom he had become quite intimate, particularly Bailey, who occupied the next bed to his in Barrack B. So eager was he to fathom the mystery, that he was tempted to make some inquiries of them ; but they might themselves be members of the Regulators. Even Bailey might belong to the potent organization, and he did not care to expose himself in the slightest

degree to their jeers or their malice. Though, as he
had been informed, there were fifty boys who had
become his enemies, and who were pledged to annoy
him to the utmost of their ability, every one seemed
to be his friend.

Hardly had he been discharged from guard duty
before his arrest was ordered, and he found himself
accused of sleeping at his post. He was conducted
to the tent of Colonel Brockridge, where the charge
was distinctly recited to him.

"What do you say to this charge, Grant? Are
you guilty or not guilty?" demanded the principal.

"Who are my accusers, sir?" asked Richard,
thinking only of the task he had laid upon himself
of discovering the Regulators.

"That does not answer my question, Grant. I
asked you whether you were guilty or not guilty,"
added the colonel, sternly.

"Not guilty, sir!" replied Richard, promptly and
firmly.

"Then you wish to have the charge proved?"

"I do, sir."

"That is rather inconvenient," said the colonel,

18 *

biting his lip. "If you are guilty, I should prefer to have you say so."

"I am not guilty, sir."

Colonel Brockridge had had too much experience with boys to neglect the looks and actions of the accused while he questioned him, for the expression often reveals more than the words. Richard's communication, on this occasion, was "yea, yea; nay, nay." He had the look of one who speaks the truth, and the principal was duly impressed by the appearance and manner of the prisoner.

"You speak very decidedly," added the colonel. "Were you at your post at half past nine o'clock?"

"I was not, sir."

"Where were you?"

Richard hesitated; there were several teachers and several company officers present. He did not like to tell the story before them, and he did not think it would be prudent to do so. Probably some of the Regulators were within hearing, and he preferred to unearth them in some other way.

"Your answer, Grant," said the principal.

"Without intending any disrespect to you, sir, I

would rather not answer," replied Richard, glancing at the officers present.

A slight curl on the lip of a cadet by the name of Rodman attracted his attention. It was a kind of suppressed sneer, which Richard interpreted that he dared not expose the doings of the secret society. His answer had been a virtual admission of the charge, and the case seemed to have gone against him. Richard concluded that the boy who could rejoice at that moment must be a Regulator.

" The penalty of sleeping at your post and deserting it would be the same; and as you admit the charge in substance, it will not be necessary to proceed any further," said Colonel Brockridge.

Richard was tempted to make a full explanation of the events of the night, but he had some doubts whether he would be believed if he did so. Besides, he was curious to know what the Regulators would do. The penalty for the offence with which he was charged could not be very heavy, and he determined to submit to it, for the purpose of exposing the Regulators at some future time.

The principal then gave him a lecture on the im-

propriety of deserting his post, when placed on guard,
explaining the consequences that might result from
such unfaithfulness in time of war. Richard listened
patiently to the reproof, and was sentenced to be confined in the guard tent for twenty-four hours.

Richard possessed his soul in patience, and slept
off a good portion of his imprisonment. He devoted
all his wakeful hours to a consideration of the doings
of the Regulators, and in devising plans for " venti-
lating " their secret proceedings.

When he was relieved from arrest, and permitted
to join his comrades, he kept a close watch upon Redman, and also upon the two privates who had been
next to him in the line on guard. They must have
been his accusers, and he was satisfied that they
belonged to the obnoxious association. Nevers, no
doubt, was also a member, and he believed him to
be the " Dobbin " of the party that had whipped
him. Here were four whom he suspected, and during the week the battalion remained in camp, their
words and their actions were carefully scanned; but
they were too adroit to expose themselves, though
Richard's close scrutiny was not entirely fruitless.

Our soldier entered heartily into the spirit of the occasion, and performed his duty with the utmost fidelity. Though he was made the victim of various petty tricks, such as smearing the stock of his musket with grease, cutting the straps of his knapsack, and hiding his blanket, he bore all these things with politic patience, and treated his comrades with the most scrupulous fairness. He was the champion of the weak, and, being the conqueror of Nevers, no one ventured to carry their opposition to his will beyond a few respectful words. He would not let a small boy be insulted or bullied; and a frown from him was generally a sufficient protection. He was foremost in all the sports of the boys, and every day increased his popularity.

If the Regulators said or did any thing to his injury, they did it very slyly, for Richard could not discover that there was any one who was not his friend. On the last day of the encampment, the election of officers was to take place, and during the week, of course there was a great deal of electioneering done for various candidates.

On the day before the election, a petition was circulated among the boys, requesting the principal to reinstate Nevers in the office from which he had been degraded. There were about fifty names on the paper when Bailey brought it to Richard. It was not very favorably received by the boys generally. Nobody could tell when or where the fifty names had been obtained; no one had seen the signers place their autographs upon the document. Richard heard Bailey and a dozen others refuse to sign it, and some of them even proposed to get up a remonstrance.

"I am going to sign the petition," said Richard, to the astonishment of his companions.

"You, Grant?" exclaimed a dozen boys, in the same breath.

"I am; just to show the fellows that I bear him no ill will," replied Richard. "Nevers was degraded for that affair with me; and, as I licked him, I think I can afford to do the handsome thing."

"Then he will be elected captain of Company D," said Bailey.

"I don't know about that," added Richard. "I am willing to see him restored to the place he was in before I came, but I shall not give him my vote for captain, or any thing else."

The victim of the Regulators took out his pencil
and wrote his name upon the petition. Though he
fully believed that Nevers was the " Dobbin " of the
party that had assaulted him, he could not prove it
and he was disposed to give him a fair chance, so
that neither he nor his friends should have any good
ground for complaint.   His example was followed
by all the boys present, and from that moment
the number of names on the paper increased very
rapidly.

At dress parade, Colonel Brockridge, to whom the
petition had been presented early in the afternoon,
called Nevers forward, and after a few remarks,
restored him to his former position as first sergeant of
Company D, observing at the same time that the
name of Richard Grant on the paper had had more
influence upon his mind than that of all the others.
It was a magnanimous act, which he heartily approved.

" Three cheers for Nevers ! " shouted some friend
of the first sergeant, when the company broke ranks.

They were given, but it was only a partial demonstration, evidently confined to about a dozen of the
company.

"Three cheers for Grant!" said Bailey, when those for the first sergeant had been given.

The call was promptly responded to, and though the cheers seemed to proceed from the entire company, there were probably about a dozen who did not join.

"Tiger!" added Bailey, with an earnestness that assured Richard he was not a member of the Regulators.

The "tiger" was added, together with a volley of applause by clapping the hands. Richard's position in Company D was not to be doubted, and the Regulators present must have felt that their influence was not very powerful.

On the following day they had a further proof of the popularity of Richard, and if they had not been very stupid, they might have seen that he had more influence than the whole band of Regulators put together. On the first ballot in Company D, the first lieutenant was elected captain; the second sergeant was elected first lieutenant. The second lieutenant was believed to be a strong friend of Nevers, and no promotion was awarded to him.

Richard Grant was elected second sergeant, and when the vote was declared, the result was greeted with a round of hearty applause. The other places were all filled, as the inclination of the majority dictated, subject only to the healthy rules of the Institute. If there had been no limit to the choice of the boys, we have no doubt their favorite would have been elected captain.

The face of Nevers was as dark as a thunder cloud after the election. The remark of Richard that he would not vote for him had been circulated through the company, and had been influential in defeating the aspirations of the first sergeant. Nevers knew very well that he owed his defeat and his restoration to his rival, whom he hated with ten fold greater vigor than before — hated him for what he had done, and hated him for what he had left undone.

Of course, Richard felt very good-natured, and snapped his fingers at the Regulators. He sat upon a stool alone after supper, thinking of his good fortune, and congratulating himself upon the skill with which he had conquered his enemies. He was satisfied that in being true to himself he had won the respect and confidence of his companions. The good resolutions he had successfully carried out had rendered him worthy of the favor bestowed upon him. In conquering himself he had conquered others.

While Richard sat on the stool thinking of the pleasant events of the day, and perhaps wondering how long it would be before he became the major of the battalion, his vanquished rival sauntered up to him, his face still looking dark and malignant.

"You have beaten me again, Grant," said he, sourly, "but your day will come soon."

"Eh, Dobbin?" replied Richard, with a good-natured smile, as he glanced at his fellow-sergeant.

"What's that?" growled Nevers. "What do you mean by calling me Dobbin?"

Richard was satisfied from the appearance of Nevers, that the name was not wholly unfamiliar to his ears. It was the first time he had ever ventured to hint at the proceedings of his first night in camp; and it was the first time that his rival had ever dared to speak to him in a surly tone.

"If you don't understand it, no matter," added Richard, with a merry twinkle of the eye.

" If you call me by that, or any other improper name, you shall suffer for it."

" How many of you will it take to punish me for it, eh, Dobbin ?"

" Dobbin again ?"

" Do you know a fellow by the name of Kennedy ?" added Richard.   " If you don't, I'll introduce you some day."

Nevers concluded that Richard was a tough customer, and he made no further allusion to any suffering in store for his defiant rival. But Richard's taunt about Kennedy, and his promises to introduce him, were not pleasant to the bully, and he walked away. He feared that the victim had been making dangerous discoveries.

On the following morning the battalion took up the line of march for the Institute, and arrived without incident or accident; and that night the boys exchanged the hard ground for the iron bed. steads in the barracks.

CHAPTER XVII.

RICHARD GIVES THE TUNBROOKERS A LESSON
IN BOATING.

AMONG the favorite recreations of the cadets of the Tunbrook Military Institute was that of boating. The beautiful lake afforded them abundant space for sailing and rowing, and quite a number of them were proficient oarsmen and excellent navigators.

On the Saturday afternoon following the return from the camp, Colonel Brockridge proposed to exercise the boys in the boats. This announcement was received with hearty applause by the cadets, and they gathered round the principal to learn the order of exercises upon the lake.

"Well, boys, suppose we appoint a couple of coxswains and have a race."

"Hurrah!" shouted the boys. "A race A race!"

"You like the plan, I see. Who shall be your leaders?" added the colonel.

The boys made no reply, but looked curiously at each other, as though they were not competent to settle the question.

"Nevers for one," said Redman.

"Very well; Nevers, we all know, is a good boatman, and has always won the races. Who shall be the other?"

No reply was made, and the principal waited some time for a suggestion.

"Grant has had considerable experience with boats, his father informed me," continued Colonel Brockridge.

"Grant! Grant!" shouted the boys.

"Grant shall be coxswain of the other boat, then. What do you say, Grant?"

"I am very willing, sir, if the fellows desire it," replied Richard, modestly.

"Very well. The race shall come off at four o'clock. Each leader shall have two hours to train his crew. The course shall be round Green Island and home, making a pull of about three miles

19 *

You shall draw lots for the choice of boats, though I don't think there is a particle of difference between them." -

The choice was between the Alice and the Emma, as the two club boats had been named. Nevers drew the first choice, and selected the Alice, and of course Richard was obliged to be satisfied with the Emma.

" The coxswains shall select their own crews. Now, draw for the first choice."

Nevers drew the prize this time also, and named Redman as his stroke oarsman. Richard took Bailey for the same station, and they continued to select alternately till each had taken his twelve oarsmen. The coxswain of the Alice had a decided advantage over his ·rival, for he had a complete knowledge of the capacity of each boy, and had before taken part in several races on the lake. Richard was aided in choosing by his friends whom he had selected, and when they stepped into the boat, he was well satisfied with his crew.

" We shall get beaten," said Bailey, in a low tone, as they shoved off the Emma.

"What makes you think so, Bailey?" demanded Richard, with a smile.

"Nevers is a great boatman. He knows all about a boat, and when he was in command he always won the race."

"Don't you croak, Bailey," laughed Richard. "I have seen a boat before to-day, and I tell you we shall not get beaten."

The coxswain spoke in a loud tone, so that all his crew could hear him, for he knew that the first requisite of success was confidence.

"I hope so," said Bailey. "I would rather any other fellow in the school should beat you than Nevers. It will be a feather in his cap."

"Don't croak, Bailey. Just believe that we shall beat, and we shall."

"I hope we shall. Nevers first got ahead of all the fellows in boating. His success elected him to his first office in the company, and if he beats you in this race, he will be captain at the next election. The boys will all stand by the fellow that beats in any thing."

"There, Bailey, if you say another word, I shall

wish I had chosen some other fellow. You will defeat us if you keep on croaking," added the coxswain, earnestly.

" I'm not croaking. I only want you to understand what you have got to do ; and I will do all I can to help you win the race. What are you going up here for ?" demanded Bailey, as the boat's bow was pointed down the river, which was the outlet of the lake.

" You ask too many questions, Bailey. If you will leave this thing to me, I will agree to whip Nevers all to pieces," said Richard, who did not like the discipline on board the Emma.

" All right, Grant. Let him alone, Bailey," said one of the boys in the middle of the boat.

" Where's the other boat ?" asked Richard. " I see her ; she has gone up the lake. That's just what I wanted her to do. I have a little business to do here before we go into the race."

He ordered the crew to cease rowing, and, to the surprise of his companions, ran the boat up to the shore. As he had intimated to them that questions were not agreeable to him, they asked none, and waited patiently till his movements should explain themselves.

"Now, Bailey, will you go up to the store-house, and bring down some black lead, and the brushes they use to clean the stoves. Don't let any body see you, and don't say a word to any one."

Bailey did not very clearly understand what this request had to do with winning the race, but he ran off with all haste to execute the mission in-trusted to him. While he was gone, Richard im-proved the opportunity to develop his system of rowing to his companions. He had attended a great many boat races on the Hudson, had belonged to a boat club in Whitestone, and had clear ideas upon all matters connected with the business of boating.

On the return of the messenger, the articles he had brought were thrown into the stern sheets. and the boat shoved off. Again, to the surprise of the crew, Richard took them down the river, half a mile, till they came to a sandy shore, where he grounded the Emma.

" Now, tumble out, fellows," said Richard, " and take your oars with you."

The boys wondered more than oefore at the singular proceedings of the coxswain, and Bailey so far overcame his respect for discipline again, as to suggest that they should have no time to practise with the oars, if they spent the precious moments in this stupid manner.

" Shut up, Bailey; I have more to lose in this race than you have," said Richard, rather curtly. " If the fellows don't believe in me for this business, I am willing to step one side, and let any other one take hold who thinks he can do it better than I can."

" Go ahead, Grant!" shouted the crew. " We are all satisfied, and so is Bailey."

" I won't speak another word, Grant," said Bailey. " I only wish I had as much confidence as you have."

" Bear a hand lively, my lads," added Richard, as he seized the painter of the boat; " I want to get her out of the water."

The boys took hold with a will, and the Emma

was soon placed high and dry upon the beach. She was then turned over.

" There, fellows," said Richard, as he pointed to the foul bottom of the boat, " do you expect to win a race with the craft in that condition ? In fifteen minutes we will have her in the water again, as clean as a lady's parlor."

By direction of the coxswain, the crew fell to scrubbing the bottom of the boat with an earnestness and zeal which soon removed every trace of moss and grass. She was then permitted to dry for a short time, and the bright October sun soon completed their work. The bottom was then covered over with black lead, and rubbed with the brushes till it shone like a newly-polished stove. The boys used their muscle upon the brushes, being relieved every minute by fresh hands.

" Now, my lads, we are in condition to win the race. Shove her off," said Richard, whose energy inspired the whole party with resolution and confidence.

The Emma was afloat again ; the boys took their places, though not till Richard had rearranged them

by their weight, so that the boat was in perfect trim
when she started.   For an hour and a half Richard
trained them in rowing, till the stroke exactly suited
him, and they fully understood all his signs and
signals.

" Now, fellows, mind your eyes, and we are' sure
to win," said the wide-awake coxswain, as the
sun fired that was to call them to the stake boat.
" I never saw a better set of rowers in my life,
and I am as well satisfied with you as though we
had been pulling together for a year."

" Bully for you, Grant," said one of the boys at
the bow.

The Emma pulled leisurely up to the large sail
boat, on board of which were the colonel, the assistant teachers, and as many of the boys as she
would comfortably accommodate.

" Are you all ready ? " shouted the colonel, as
the Alice and the Emma took their stations.

" All ready, sir," replied Richard, cheerfully.

" All ready, sir," added Nevers, confidently.

Both parties were impatient for the contest to
begin, and both were almost certain of winning

the victory. Even the boats seemed to share in the spirit of their crews, and anxious to have the fetters removed that they might bound away upon the errand of conquest. Each had appropriate flags at the bow and stern, and one with a taste for boats would have been delighted by the appearance of the trim craft.

" Ready for the signal!" shouted the colonel again.

" Down with that flag in the bow, Carter," said Richard to the bowman, as he took down the color in the stern.

" What's that for?" asked one of the crew of the Emma.

" They hold the wind, and keep us back a little. We will be on the safe side. Now, ready, fellows, and mind what I have said to you. Don't look at the other boat till you can see her over our stern."

Nevers disdained to follow the example of his rival in removing his flags, saying that he could beat him with his colors flying. Nevers prided himself upon his skill in handling a boat, and he felt that the opportunity had come which would enable him to triumph over the hated usurper, as he considered Richard. He knew how much glory and honor would be awarded to the conqueror in this race, and that if he could beat his rival, scores of those fair-weather friends, who always attach themselves to a rising man, would leave him.

The signal gun was on shore, and at a gesture from the colonel, it was discharged. The report seemed to unloose the bonds which chained the boats to their stations, and they bounded away. The crew of the Alice bent to their oars with the most tremendous energy, while that of the Emma seemed to be inspired by the cool and steady nerve of her coxswain. They had been fully and thoroughly instructed in their duty.

The crowd of boys on the shore were silent and breathless with the interest they felt in the exciting race; and when, before the boats had gone a quarter of a mile, they discovered the Alice more than half a length ahead of her companion, the jaws of Richard's friends dropped, and their faces were

as long as though a ten pound weight had been
fastened to the chin of each, while a smile of tri-
umphant satisfaction lighted up the faces of Nevers's well-wishers.

" Nevers has it ! " exclaimed one of his intimates,
as, when she rounded Green Island, the Alice was
found to be more than a length ahead of the
Emma.

" Not yet," said one of the other clique. " Let
Dick Grant alone. He knows what he is about.
He don't half try yet."

The crew of the Emma could not yet see the
Alice over the stern of the boat, and we doubt
not they shared the anxiety and despondency of
their friends on shore. But no sooner had the
boats rounded the island, and commenced on the
home stretch, than Richard's vibrating body began
gradually to move more rapidly, and just in pro-
portion as he increased the movement, the Emma
lessened the distance between herself and the
Alice.

" Steady, fellows ; don't get excited. Dip a little
deeper," said Richard, in a quiet, cool tone. " We

are doing splendidly, and you shall see the Alice
over the stern in about three minutes."

Nevers, as in the fight with his rival, began to
be very much excited when he saw that he was
losing ground. He spoke quick and earnest words
to the crew of his boat, who had been doing their
utmost from the beginning, urging them to increase
their exertions. Richard had not permitted his
crew to do their best at first, but had kept in their
muscles a reserve of strength for the final emergency. The party in the Alice had no such reserve
power, and their efforts to increase the speed of
the boat were put forth at the expense of a proper
attention to skill and precision.

The boats were now side by side, and they continued in this relative position until they were
within half a mile of the stake boat. The race
had become intensely exciting, and again the two
cliques on shore were breathless and silent with
interest. Neither party had any thing to indicate
the success of its favorite.

Even yet Richard had not put his crew to their
utmost. But the decisive moment had arrived, and

his body began to sway backward and forward
with increasing rapidity, and a quarter of a mile
more gave him half a boat-length's advantage over
his rival.

"Steady, fellows; keep cool," said he, in a loud
whisper. "Don't miss a stroke, and make every one
tell all it will. Now you see her over the stern
— but pull steady."

The Emma was a length ahead of the Alice
when Richard finished these remarks. The boats
were within an eighth of a mile of the end of the
course, and the murmuring applause of the Grant
party on shore began to reach the ears of the
contestants.

"Pull! Pull!" shouted Nevers, filled with rage
and vexation. "Pull with all your might, fellows.
We can beat him yet, if you only stick to it"

He increased the rapidity of his motions, but
his crew were unable to keep up with him. Their
stroke was unsteady; some of them forgot to feather
their oars, and some scarcely dipped the blades in
the water.

"Steady!" said Richard, with more energy

20 *

'Mind your stroke. Keep both eyes on me Here we are!" shouted he, jumping up from his seat in the stern, and giving the order to cease rowing.

The Emma flew by the stake boat two and a half lengths ahead of the Alice, and a stunning roar of cheers from the shore and the sail boat saluted the victors.

" Grant forever ! Three cheers for Grant!" shouted Bailey, as the crew of the Emma rose and made the welkin ring with their huzzas.

CHAPTER XVIII.

RICHARD WINS ANOTHER RACE, AND TUNBROOK IS MUTINOUS.

IT was a proud moment for Richard Grant when he rose from the stern sheets of the Emma, and found the Alice was two or three lengths behind, and when he heard the shouts of his friends rend the air. It was victory — another triumph over the Regulators, who had threatened to make Tunbrook too hot to hold him. They did not get ahead very fast, and he felt that his conquest over them was complete.

The hour of prosperity, of triumph, is the most dangerous period in the experience of a young man. He is on the top of the wave, and he sees not the dark abyss that yawns on either side of him. Truly we need adversity to keep us from forgetting God and duty; to keep us from forgetting that truth and justice are more mighty than mere success.

But when Richard came to Tunbrook, he came with a solemn resolution to forsake the error of his ways, and find happiness in the path of recti- tude. Whatever success had attended him, he attributed to the influence of this good resolution. He had manfully resisted temptation; he had cured himself of several bad habits, and he had made good progress in the conquest of himself. He had often felt an inclination to resent with hard words and heavy blows the sneers of the Nevers faction, but he had controlled himself; and each victory of principle over inclination had made him stronger in his purpose to do right.

Bertha's answer to his letter, in which he had informed her of his election to the post of sergeant, cautioned him against being too much elated by his good fortune. She hoped his promotion would not make him think too much of himself. When he realized that he had won a new victory, when he heard the boys shouting his name, the words of his sister came to his mind, and he determined

to bear his honors meekly, and to feel kindly towards
Nevers and his friends.

As they pulled to the stake boat, Richard cautioned his crew not to "crow" over the fellows in
the other boat, for it was a friendly contest, and
he did not wish to see any ill feeling on either
side. The Alice was already alongside the sail
boat. Nevers was in no enviable frame of mind;
he looked dark and sour, and Richard only bestowed one glance upon him, lest his looks should
be misconstrued.

"Grant, you have won the race," said Colonel
Brockridge, as the Emma came up. "I had no
idea of such a result."

"Three cheers for Grant!" shouted an enthusiastic boy in the sail boat.

"No," added the principal, as he glanced at the
crest-fallen coxswain of the Alice, and saw that he
was taking his defeat very hardly. "You have
cheered enough. We don't want any unkind feelings to grow out of this affair. Nevers, you have
been beaten, but —"

"I shouldn't have been, if I had had fair play,"

growled Nevers, whose anger was manifest in his
tones.

"Has there been any foul play?" demanded the
colonel.

"Yes, sir, there has," replied Nevers, sharply.

"What was it?"

"The fellows in the Emma took her out of the
water, cleaned her, and covered her bottom with
black lead."

"I don't see any unfair play in that. You had
the right to use your time for preparation as you
wished," said the principal.

"He couldn't have beaten if his boat hadn't
been in better condition," added Nevers.

"It is a good driver that keeps his horse in
good condition. I think it is rulable for each crew
to prepare their boat as they think best."

"Well, he beat us by a trick. What did they
go down the river for to haul up their boat?"

"That is their business. I see you are not satisfied, Nevers."

"No, sir, I am not. I like to have fair play in
these things."

"So do I," said the colonel, with a quiet smile, "and I think you had better try this thing over again. Now, suppose you exchange boats, and pull round once more, that we may see how much good the black lead did. What do you say, Grant?"

"I am willing, sir," replied Richard.

"We are all fagged out, now, sir," interposed Nevers.

"I proposed this method to remove your objections to the race, Nevers. You might have cleaned your boat, if you had been so disposed."

"I didn't think of it," snarled Nevers.

"If a general should get beaten because he did not think to bring up his ammunition, or by neglecting any precaution, his want of forethought would hardly be deemed a sufficient excuse. I should like to have you exchange boats for a short pull, if you don't go round the island."

"We are tired out, sir."

"The other crew have pulled the same distance you have," added the principal.

"Try it, Nevers, try it," whispered Redman. "We shall be laughed at for a month, if we don't. We will whip them this time."

"I am willing to try it, sir," said Nevers, though his words belied his feelings.

Both crews were somewhat rested from the fatigue of the race, and they exchanged places in the two boats, taking the positions assigned to them.

"We shall get beat this time, sure," said Bailey.

"No, we won't," replied Richard.

"Well, if you say so, then we shall not. It would be the greatest thing that ever was, if we should whip them again. It will show that black lead isn't a great institution, after all."

"No, it won't. Those fellows don't pull worth a cent. If they can't do better than they did before, we shall whip them all to pieces. Now, mind what I told you; don't hurry, and keep cool."

The signal was given, and the two boats dashed off. The race was very nearly a repetition of the first one. Richard kept a sufficient quantity of muscle in reserve for the last half mile of the race, and came in about a boat length ahead of the Emma. The one and a half length's difference in the two races seemed precisely to indicate the amount of virtue in black lead.

RICHARD WINS THE RACE   Page 240

Again the thundering cheers of the Grant party reverberated over the lake and through the grove. Nevers was astonished, as well as angry, and his face was darker than ever.

" Are you satisfied now, Nevers ? " asked the colonel, when the Alice and the Emma came alongside the stake boat.

" Yes, sir," replied he, desperately ; " but I don't understand it."

" I do," said the principal. " The other crew pull better than yours. I never saw better pulling in my life than those fellows showed us. I hope there is no hard feeling between you."

" No, sir," replied Nevers; but his looks and his tones belied his words.

" He will pull us all down at this rate," muttered Redman, as the Emma left the stake boat.

" Something must be done," added Nevers. " He has got half the fellows on his side now."

" What shall we do ? " asked Redman, who seemed to regard it as a hopeless case.

" We'll fix him yet."

Some earnest conversation followed these remarks.

21

It was carried on in whispers, and entirely suspended when the Alice approached. The boats were secured, and both crews landed.

" Grant, you have beaten me fairly, and there is my hand," said Nevers, when the two coxswains met on shore.

Richard was utterly confounded by this show of good will on the part of his rival. He took the proffered hand, and gave it a hearty pressure.

"Thank you, Nevers; it is very kind of you to treat me in this handsome manner. I'm sure I don't feel any ill will toward you," replied Richard.

" We will be friends, Grant, and perhaps you will tell me how this thing was done ? "

" With the greatest pleasure."

" You have some secret in rowing."

" I will tell you all I know about it, any time you please," said Richard, frankly.

" Thank you ; you are the first fellow that ever beat me rowing, and I honor you for it, but I don't understand it. Shall we be friends now, Grant ? "

" With all my heart."

Richard could not have been more astonished if the sky had fallen, than he was when his great enemy approached him with words of kindness and conciliation. He could scarcely believe his senses ; but there was Nevers by his side, as good-natured as though he had won the race ; and more than this, the rival crews were suddenly on the most excellent terms, and were fraternizing like brothers. Nevers had evidently given up the point, and intended to withdraw all . opposition to the advancement of Richard.

Nevers and his friends seemed to be sincere, and the hatchet appeared to have been actually buried. Richard was so well treated by them, that he came to the conclusion that the Regulators had been dissolved, or at least that they had turned their attention to some more promising field of labor.

On the first of November, when the boys assembled for morning prayers, the principal announced a new regulation, requiring every member of the Institute to be in-doors during the off time, from seven till nine in the evening. Before, they had been permitted to go where they pleased during

these hours, as long as they did not leave the estate.
But some of the boys had been seen in the village
of Tunbrook after eight in the evening; and all
efforts to discover who they were had been una-
vailing. The prohibition had been made to correct
this evil.

When the new regulation was announced, there
was a general murmur of disapprobation among the
students, for some of their best sport had been
enjoyed out of doors, after dark. No one ventured
to remonstrate, but the order was exceedingly unpopular.

" I won't stand it," said one and another, during
the first recreation hour in the afternoon. " It's too
bad; it will spoil all our fun."

" The fellows are all agreed on this point," said
Redman.

" I am willing to observe all reasonable regulations, but we might as well go into a monastery
as submit to this thing," added Nevers. " What
do you say, Grant ? "

" I don't like it. We intended to have a first
rate game of foot ball these moonlight evenings."

" There isn't a fellow in the school that likes
it," said Redman.

" That's so," replied Bailey. " I don't see the
use of the rule either."

" Nor I."

" Some of the fellows have been down to Tunbrook almost every night."

" What's that to us, as long as we didn't go?"
said Bailey. " The innocent ought not to be punished with the guilty."

" The colonel couldn't find out who they were,"
said Redman, with a kind of chuckle. " No fellow would 'blow' on the others."

" It is easy enough to talk," said Bailey, " but
what are you going to do?"

" Do? Why, resist it, of course," replied Redman. " I am ready to do so, for one. Let us all
stay out to-night till nine o'clock."

" Agreed," added some of the larger boys.

" We shall get punished if we do," suggested
Bailey.

" No matter. They will have to punish the

21 *

whole crowd. The guard house won't hold us all,"
replied Redman.

"Let us have a plan about it. We will get up
a regular mutiny," said Nevers. "If we can get
a hundred fellows to go with us, we shall make the
old man cave in."

"Good, Nevers! Let all the fellows that will
join meet under the big oak by the river, at five
o'clock, or as soon as we get out of school. Let
each fellow talk it round in a quiet way, but don't
let the teachers hear a word."

"Will you be there, Grant?" asked Nevers.

"I don't know. I will see."

"Don't know?" said Nevers. "Don't you see
all the fellows are in for it?"

"I will think of it," replied Richard, as he
walked away.

CHAPTER XIX.

RICHARD IS DETERMINED, AND SOME ALLUSION IS MADE TO " WATERMELONS."

THERE had been a time when Richard Grant would have desired no better fun than to engage in such a mutiny as that proposed by Nevers and Redman; and he was not yet so far removed from his evil propensities as to be able to decline the proposition. The boys of the Institute believed they had a real grievance, for it seemed harsh and needless to deprive them of some of their best hours for amusement. It looked just as though the principal was angry because he could not ascertain who had broken the rules of the school, and spitefully intended to punish the innocent with the guilty.

Probably none of them intended to carry their opposition any farther than to express their disapprobation of the new regulation. The colonel was

a universal favorite, and they had full confidence
in his judgment and his justice. Perhaps the desire to have a little fun and excitement was the
strongest motive that actuated them.

During the afternoon, the plan to redress their
grievance was whispered among the boys. "All
the fellows were going to join the mutiny" was
the strongest inducement that could be used to
obtain the consent of the timid ones; and if "all
were going to join," it would require a great deal
of moral courage to stand aloof from the scheme.

Richard was sorely perplexed. With the others,
he felt that the new regulation was arbitrary and
unnecessary; and such a scrape as the boys proposed was exactly in accordance with his antece-
dents. He wanted to join for the fun of the thing,
and because the rest of the boys were going to do
so. He did not like to be singular. Besides, he
might injure his popularity, and lose some of the
influence he possessed, if he refused to join.

The temptation was so strong that he could not
at first resist it; and though he did not positively
promise to meet the others under the big oak, he

gave them some encouragement that he would do
so. The little time he had to think of the matter
during the study and recreation hours did not enable him to arrive at a conclusion; and at five
o'clock, when school was dismissed, he was still
halting between two opinions.

When he left the school room, he fixed his mind
upon the question, and began to discuss it in the
most vigorous manner. He knew that any resistance to the authorities of the school was wrong.
Colonel Brockridge had made the rule, and it was
his duty to observe it. What would Bertha say,
after he had given her such a glowing account of
his success in overcoming temptation, when she was
informed that he had joined a mutiny?

" I'll keep my resolution ! " said he, stamping
his foot upon the ground to emphasize his determination. " I'll stand out against the whole of
them."

Half past five came, and nearly every boy in the
school had gone to the appointed place. Richard
sat on the bench at the foot of the flagstaff on
the parade ground, thinking whether his duty

required him to do any thing more than simply
refuse to join the mutiny. Somehow, it entered
into his head that it was his duty to prevent the
rebellion if he could. It even occurred to him that
he ought to inform Colonel Brockridge of the intention of the students, and thus place himself on
the side of law and order; but he rejected this
suggestion, it was so utterly repugnant to his nature. He could not "tell tales out of school."
If any body's life, property, or happiness had been
at stake, he might have felt differently. Richard
was a novice in advocating the claims of law and
order, of truth and justice; and he was more easily
satisfied than some would have been in a similar
situation.

While he was debating this matter with himself, ,
Nevers, Bailey, and Redman approached, and inter-
rupted his meditations. They appeared to be a
committee appointed to wait upon him, and ascertain his views upon the momentous question.

"You didn't come down," said Nevers.

"No: I have concluded not to join in the scrape,"
replied Richard, gravely.

" Why not ? "

" Because I don't think it is right ; and I think if we speak to the colonel about the matter, he will make it all right."

" I tell you, Grant, he has no right to make such a regulation," added Nevers, with energy ; "and I, for one, am not going to beg him not to do that which he has no right to do."

" Come, Grant, you are almost the only fellow in the school who won't join the mutiny," said Redman.

" The fellows are all in for it, and you had better come," added Bailey.

" No ; I won't join," replied Richard, decidedly.

" Come down to the grove, whether you join or not," suggested Nevers.

" I am willing to go down to the grove, but I shall not go in for this scrape."

" Come along, then."

The boys walked over to the grove, the committee using all their eloquence and logic to induce Richard to change his mind ; but thus far he remained firm and loyal to his good resolution. His arrival at the grove created a sensation, for it seemed to be evidence that he was to form one of the party.

The position of Richard Grant on the present occasion was so novel that he could hardly believe in his own identity. Like the old woman with the little pig, it did not seem to be he that was refusing an invitation to join in a scrape so harmless as the one proposed ; and he almost needed an introduction to himself.

But Richard was himself, truly himself — himself in the highest and noblest sense. His determination to keep his resolution seemed to create around him an atmosphere of purity, and the more he breathed it, the firmer and the stronger he became. The boys exhorted him singly, in couples, and by squads, to join the foolish enterprise, but without effect.

" Better come with us, Grant," said Nevers. " We have got a first-rate plan, and we shall have a tip-top time."

" I have fully made up my mind not to go," replied Richard.

" I shall not go, if Grant doesn't," added Bailey.

" Nor I," said another.

" Back out — will you ? " sneered Nevers, his face darkening with an expression of anger.

" I said I would join if Grant did," replied Bailey, stung by the reproach.

Most of the boys were silent for a time, for the decided and unexpected stand taken by Richard, the favorite of the school, altered the complexion of the whole affair. This silence was succeeded by a more unequivocal demonstration. One after another followed the example of Bailey, and deserted the bad cause, till Richard found himself no longer alone, but supported by at least thirty of the best fellows in the Institute; and then they began to come over in squads.

" You are the meanest set of cowards I ever saw in my life," exclaimed Nevers, bitterly, when the enterprise appeared to be fully nipped in the bud.

" Grant is right," several of the boys replied.

" Grant ! " sneered Nevers, angrily. " He wasn't always so nice as he is now."

" That's so," said Redman, as he placed himself

by the side of the bully. "We know a thing or two about Grant, before he became pious."

"What do you mean by pious?" demanded Richard, stepping up to the speaker; and as he did so, his fists were involuntarily clinched.

"Watermelons!" replied Redman, vindictively.

"Watermelons!" added Nevers.

"Watermelons!" responded a dozen or more of the large boys, who had gathered around Redman.

"Do you walk in your sleep any now, Grant?" said Redman, with a mocking laugh. "You wasn't pious *then*."

Richard was so mortified and confused by these taunts that he wished the earth might open and hide him from the exulting gaze of his assailants. His blood boiled with shame and indignation, and more than ever before he realized that "the way of the transgressor is hard." His first impulse was to rush upon his dastardly foes, and crush them beneath the weight of his strong arm.

Most of the boys looked at each other with astonishment, wondering what could be meant by "watermelons," and walking in his sleep. It was evident to Richard that only a few of his companions understood the reflections cast upon him. There he stood, trembling, as it were, in the balance, and ready to be carried up or down by this new and most terrible trial — up into a higher sphere of virtue, or down into a deeper degradation than any he had yet fathomed.

"J will be true to myself!" said he to himself, after he had stood silent for a moment, blushing with shame, and assailed by the foe without and the foe within.

His clinched fist unclosed, the muscles relaxed, and though his face was still red, a smile of triumph played upon his lips.

"Will you go, Watermelons?" sneered Redman.

"I will not," replied Richard.

"Shut up, Redman," interposed Nevers, who entirely mistook the singular change which had come over Richard's countenance. "Come, Grant, you and I will talk it over alone;" and he took his arm, and led him away from the crowd,

"You see we know all about these things," continued Nevers, "but we don't want to be hard upon you. Only about a dozen of us know any thing about those scrapes."

"Who told you about them?" asked Richard.

"That's nothing to the purpose. You are a good fellow, Grant, and I advise you to join us; if you do, not a fellow shall ever say a word about watermelons or sleep-walking."

"I will not join you, whatever you say and whatever you do."

"Then you won't hear any thing but watermelons while you stay here. I called you out as a friend, and I think you had better go with us."

"I will not."

"Then we will tell all the fellows."

"I will save you the trouble by telling them myself."

"Come, Grant."

"I will not."

"Go it, then, Watermelons!" said Nevers, as he ran back to the others, and told them of the result of the interview.

Richard wondered who could have informed them of his scrapes, but he could form no idea. Lest our readers should be equally in the dark, we will tell them, confidentially, that Sandy Brimblecom had done the mischief. A cousin of his, on his way to Tunbrook, had stopped a day in White-stone. This relative was, unfortunately, one of the Nevers' faction, and the information he brought was carefully preserved for an emergency.

"All who join, come under the big tree!" shouted Redman. "If you walk in your sleep, Grant, perhaps you will pay us a visit."

"Asleep or awake," replied Richard, calmly, but forcibly, "I shall know enough to keep out of bad company."

"Do you mean me by that?" demanded Red-man, rushing up to Richard, and shaking his fist in his face.

"I do."

"Then take that;" and Redman struck Richard in the face.

The latter did take that, but the next instant his assailant lay upon the ground, where Richard with a single blow had thrown him.

22 *

" None of that, Redman," interposed Nevers.
" The colonel will be down upon us."

" Let's lick him," said another.

" I am ready," coolly replied Richard, throwing
off his coat.

But prudence carried the day, and the mutineers
retired to the big oak. Only about fifty, or one
fourth of, the students, responded to the call of Redman, and the rest retired from the ground.

" What did they mean by ' watermelons' ? " asked
Bailey, as they walked up to the Institute.

" I'll tell you all about it ; " replied `Richard.
" I got into some scrapes before I came here ; "
and he told his companions the whole story. " But,
fellows, I have turned over a new leaf."

" Good ! " said Bailey. " I am glad you told
us ; and I'm sure no decent fellow in the Institute
will ever fling it at you."

Richard felt better when he had told the whole
truth. He confided in his friends, and feared no
his enemies. When they reached the parade ground
they saw that the mutineers had taken possession
of every one of the boats, and were sailing up the

lake towards Green Island. They dared not return to the Institute, fearing that their plan might be discovered.

Richard was informed that arrangements had been made before he joined them ; that they intended to take all the boats, so that the instructors could not reach them, and encamp on the island.

When the rolls were called, the absence of about fifty of the boys was discovered by the teachers. The truth came out, and the sharp eye of Colonel Brockridge seemed to glow with unwonted lustre.

CHAPTER XX.

RICHARD VISITS GREEN ISLAND, AND THE REGU-
LATORS CONSIDER THEIR PLANS.

THE evening exercises proceeded as usual, no
allusion whatever being made to the absence of
the mutineers, after the facts had been revealed.
But no one supposed that the energetic principal
would drop the matter where it then stood.

Richard had been "putting that and that together" since the events which had transpired in
the grove, till he was pretty well satisfied that the
mutineers now upon Green Island were the Regulators. The evidences which led him to this conclusion had been carefully collected from the time
he had been whipped by them in the woods near
the camp. Though Nevers had appeared to be
very friendly since the race, his conduct had not
been above suspicion.

During the evening the boys had a great deal to say about the mutiny, and some of them even regretted that they had not joined, especially as the colonel did not seem to care much about the affair. About eight o'clock in the evening, Richard was sent for by the principal.

"Grant," said Colonel Brockridge, as Richard entered the office, "I have heard all about your conduct, and I wish to express to you my approbation. You have, indeed, turned over a new leaf, as you told the boys, and I congratulate you upon your success in keeping your good resolution. I have just written a letter to your father, which you may read."

The principal handed him the letter, and with a glow of pride and satisfaction, Richard read the high commendation which was bestowed upon him. There was no allusion to the affair of the day, and the praise covered his general conduct since he had been at Tunbrook.

"I learn hat you have been true to yourself, and true to the rules of the Institute, under peculiar trials. I sympathize with you. But you have won the respect and regard of all the good boys. You can afford to be disliked by the others."

" I have tried to do my duty, sir," replied Rich. ard, blushing at the praise bestowed upon him.

" You have done well. I know how fond you are of exciting adventure, and I wonder that you had the strength to resist this temptation."

" I am surprised myself," added Richard.

" If I except the fight, which was greatly palliated by the circumstances, and the sleeping on guard when we were in camp, your conduct has been entirely unexceptio.iable since you came to the Institute. Sleeping on gaurd is not — "

" I didn't sleep on guard, sir," interposed Richard, mildly and respectfully. "I am prepared to explain all about that now."

" Indeed ? It is rather late now," said the principal, shaking his head.

" I think I have unearthed the Regulators."

" The Regulators ? I haven't heard any thing of them for a year. I supposed they no longer existed."

" They do exist," added Richard. " I happen to know something about them."

" What do you know ? "

In reply to this question, Richard narrated all the particulars of his abduction from his post while doing guard duty.

" But why didn't you tell me about this ? " demanded the colonel, surprised and indignant at the audacity of the Regulators. " Why did you suffer the penalty of ‘deserting your post, when you were innocent ? "

" I thought it would be better in the end, sir. I wanted to find out who the Regulators were."

" Well, have you found out ? "

" I think I have, sir."

" Who are they ? "

" I am pretty well satisfied that they are encamped upon Green Island just now," said Richard, with a smile.

" What evidence have you ? "

Richard stated, at considerable length, the facts and incidents which had led him to this conclusion: but the colonel was not fully satisfied.

" If you will permit me, sir, I think I could prove what I say to your entire satisfaction."

" What do you wish to do ? "

" I wish to visit Green Island," replied Richard, boldly.

" They would whip you again."

" I am not afraid of them."

" How will you get over to the island ? The young rascals have taken all the boats."

" I can borrow a skiff; if not, I can go over on a plank."

" But they would handle you rather roughly."

" I don't intend to let them see me. I think I can manage the matter, sir."

" Well, Grant, your plan will harmonize with mine. I intend to punish these mutineers, as they foolishly call themselves, in a novel way; and I have already made my arrangements to do so. But you shall carry out your scheme first."

" I should be very glad to do so, and I am confident that I shall succeed."

" You shall try it, at all events."

" Will you let Bailey go with me ? " asked Richard.

" No; I do not wish to expose him to danger.

You can take care of yourself, it appears, if you get into trouble. Do you want some one with you ?"

"I think it would be better."

"Mr. Gault shall accompany you, but you shall manage the matter yourself."

"Very well, sir. What shall I do for a boat ?"

"You shall have one of the pontoon boats. It will be better than a skiff."

"Good! I didn't think of that," said Richard, with enthusiasm.

"Now, Grant, not a word must be said of the events of to-night."

It was after nine o'clock when this conference was finished, and the boys had retired. Richard and the principal left the office, and repaired to the stables, where they found three of the instruct-ors, including Mr. Gault. The horses were attached to the pontoon wagon, ready for a start. The whole party seated themselves in the vehicle, and were driven by the public road to a spot near the shore of the lake. One of the rubber boats was unloaded, and Mr. Gault and Richard carried it down to the bank.

23

The night was cloudy and dark. Green Island was half a mile from the place where they proposed to embark, and there was no danger that the mutineers would see or hear them. The boat was filled with air, by the aid of a bellows, and placed in the water. Richard requested Mr. Gault to lie down in the boat, and, with a short paddle he had brought for the purpose, he propelled the light craft towards her destination.

The utmost care and quiet were necessary to prevent the mutineers from gaining any knowledge of the movement; and when the boat was within a few rods of the island, Richard laid aside his paddle and listened. He could hear the Regulators talking and laughing at some distance from the shore, and he soon satisfied himself that no sentinels had been detached to guard the approaches. With a few strokes of his paddle, he brought the boat alongside the island.

Richard seemed to be a master of strategy, and conducted his movements with such skill and prudence, that he and Mr. Gault succeeded in effecting a landing without disturbing the mutineers.

" Now, sir, we must lie down and crawl upon
the ground till we get within hearing distance of
them," whispered Richard.

" I will follow you, Grant," replied the instructor.

" We must move very slowly."

" There is plenty of time."

Richard led the way, crawling like a snake upon
the grass, so slowly and so cautiously that not a
particle of noise seemed to be made.   Near the
centre of the island there was a clump of trees,
which had been dignified by the title of a grove.
The mutineers were seated upon the ground in
this place.   Though the distance to the grove from
the place where Mr. Gault and Richard had landed .
was only a few rods, more than half an hour was
consumed in reaching a spot which would be near
enough to enable them to hear what was said.

The deep gloom beneath a spreading oak afforded
them a friendly shelter ; and here they disposed of
themselves to the best advantage to effect the object in view.   For half an hour they listened to
conversation on all topics.   Various wild schemes

were proposed to bring the colonel to terms. Some declared their intention to spend a week on the island.

" We should freeze and starve," said another.

" No ; Leslie — I mean Kennedy — said he would supply us with food ; and we can make a tent of the sails of the boat."

" Let us stick together, whatever we do," added another. " If we could only have got Grant over here, we should have fixed him."

" Thank you," said Richard to himself; and he listened to this kind of talk for some time, beginning to fear that he should not obtain the information for which he came.

" Regulators, come to order !" said Nevers, at last, much to the satisfaction of the listeners. " Are all present Regulators ?"

" They are," replied Redman.

" Guards, to your stations."

Richard could not see where their stations were; and he hoped the line of their duty would not lead them to the oak under which Mr. Gault and himself were seated.

"It is a long time since we have had a chance to hold a regular meeting; and it may be a long time before we are able to do so again. Perhaps it was lucky that all except the Regulators backed out," continued Nevers. "You all know the business we have on our hands."

"We do," replied several.

"By a judicious use of *watermelons* and *sleep-walking*, we shall accomplish our purpose," continued Nevers.

"We must do it before the next election, my chief," said Redman.

"It is of no use to attempt to whip him, or any thing of that sort," answered "my chief," which seemed to be the official designation of the presiding officer.

"I have a plan which I think will procure his expulsion from the school."

"State it; and every Regulator will remember the penalty of disclosing one of the society's secrets."

"He shall be pounded till he is black and blue," said the members, in concert.

"And every Regulator shall despise him as man
and boy, to the end of his life."

"That's so," responded the members.

"Go on, Redman," said the chief.

"Next Sunday night, the sheds, near the grove,
will be set on fire. On Friday night Grant's French
exercise book will be taken from his desk. He
will fail in his lesson on Saturday, and the colonel
must punish him. This will make him mad. The
exercise book will be torn up, and pieces of it,
especially the cover with his name on it, will be
found near the burnt building. Masters, who is
on good terms with Grant, on a certain pretence,
known to him and me, will induce him to wait at
the shed until after dark, where he will be seen
by Mr. Gault, when he goes his rounds. A broken
bunch of matches will be found in Grant's closet,
where no fellow is allowed to keep matches. Other
suspicious circumstances will appear at the time
for they are in charge of proper persons."

"You hear," said the chief.

"I don't like the plan," said one.

"Nor I," chimed in a dozen others.

" It is a mean thing," added the first objector.

" How many officers has the Society of Regulators ? " demanded the chief, sternly.

" One, whom all obey," replied the members.

" Who is he ? "

" Nevers."

" I am chief, and I command that this be done,"
said the chief.

Twenty or thirty of the members, as Richard judged
by the voices, protested against the scheme ; but the
measure was ordered in spite of this opposition.

" Is there a traitor here ? " demanded the chief.

" Not one," replied the members.

The chief then urged the necessity of using
strong measures. He pointed out the danger of
permitting Grant to remain in the school ; and the
plan would insure his expulsion. But still the in-
tractable ones objected, and their names were ordered to be given. As they were announced, Mr.
Gault, aided by faith rather than sight, wrote them
down on the back of some letters he had in his
pocket. The business was finished, and it was proposed to establish a watch on the island for the night

"We must go," whispered Richard; and he crawled off, followed by Mr. Gault.

They reached the water without being discovered, and embarked in the rubber boat.

"If they place sentinels on the watch, the colonel's plan will be defeated," said Mr. Gault.

"What is his plan?"

"To get all the boats away from them, and keep them on the island till they have had enough of it."

"We must do it before the watch is set," added Richard.

To accomplish this purpose, he paddled the float to the place where the boats were moored, and cast them all adrift. The slight current of the lake carried them slowly down to the river, and the listeners returned to the shore, and reported what they had done to the colonel. The whole party were then driven round to the outlet of the lake, where they secured the boats as they floated down.

The business of the night was done, and the party retired to their several apartments.

CHAPTER XXI.

RICHARD ANNIHILATES THE REGULATORS, AND THE STORY IS CONCLUDED.

IT would have damaged the self-esteem of the Regulators if they could have seen how little notice was taken of their absence at the Institute on the day following the development of the mutiny. Every thing went on as usual, and the instructors did not even allude to the rebels or the rebellion. It seemed to be the policy of the principal to maintain a " masterly inactivity " in regard to them.

Perhaps Colonel Brockridge was not so indifferent as he appeared to be. He had stationed men on both sides of the lake to prevent any communication between the mutineers and persons on the shore At noon it was reported that a boy by the name of Leslie, who lived in Tunbrook, and who had been expelled from the Institute, had attempted to visit the island. Richard was curious to know who Leslie was, for he had heard the name mentioned by the Regulators.

The first day of November was very mild and pleasant. It was one of the sweet days of the Indian summer, and the rebels on Green Island were highly favored by this circumstance. On the second day the wind changed, and it blew clear and cold from the north-west. Just before sunset, a white flag was seen upon a pole, near the landing place on the island. Colonel Brockridge was informed of the fact, and the large sail boat was sent off to relieve the rebels from their uncomfortable situation.

Richard and two of the instructors were deputed to visit the island, and ascertain the import of the " flag of truce." The teachers were not boatmen, and our hero was the only person available as a navigator; and he was too deeply interested in the fate of the Regulators to be averse to the visit.

On arriving at the island, the rebels were found to be in a very deplorable condition. They had eaten nothing since dinner on the preceding day, and were shivering with cold. Mr. Gault calmly inquired what they wanted.

"We want to return," replied Nevers, whose teeth chattered as he spoke.

"Step into the boat, then."

But the boat would not carry them all, and it was necessary to make two trips to convey the entire .party. On the passage, Richard attended . closely to his duty, and did not speak a word to the rebels. The two instructors were as taciturn as the boatman.

The party seemed to be astonished that their return created no sensation. No restraint was placed upon them, and when they. landed each went where he chose, but most of them found their way to the warm rooms of the Institute.

"Have you had a pleasant time, Nevers?" asked the colonel, when he met the chief of the Regulators.

"Not very, sir," replied Nevers, with a ghastly smile.

This was all the allusion that was made to the affair. Provisions disappeared with astonishing ra-

pidity at the supper table that night. The Regulators looked very tame and "chapfallen" for a
day or two; and Nevers condescended to inform
Richard that the whole thing was a bad failure.

Colonel Brockridge had requested Mr. Gault and
Richard to be entirely silent in regard to what had
transpired while they were upon the island. He
did not explain his purpose to Richard, but his in-
junction was faithfully observed.

The Regulators, even to Nevers and Redman,
were very cordial and considerate towards their
intended victim, and Richard believed they had
abandoned their wicked purpose, till, on Saturday
morning, he missed his French exercise book. Without it, he could not recite his lesson, and he was
checked for the failure, and reported to Colonel
Brockridge. The principal sent for him, and every
boy in school supposed he was under censure for
the deficiency.

On Sunday night, when the boys were permitted to walk, Masters told Richard that Bailey
wished to see him on particular business near the
Grove shed, as the building was called. Richard

promised to meet him at the place assigned. He waited there some time, but as Bailey did not come, he returned to the parlor of the Institute. He met Bailey here, and asked if he wished to see him.

" Yes; I wanted to show you something in the shed, but it will do just as well in the morning," replied Bailey, somewhat to the astonishment of Richard, who, of course, understood what all these things were for.

" What was it?" asked the intended victim.

" It was a piece of your exercise book; and I didn't know but the piece might enable you to find the whole."

While they were talking the alarm of fire was given; but before they could reach the spot, some ready hands had extinguished the flames. In accordance with the programme laid down upon the island, pieces of Richard's exercise book, some of them half burned, were found in and near the shed. Several cards of matches, and half the printed paper that had enclosed the original bunch,

24

were also picked up near the building which had been devoted to destruction.

An investigation was immediately commenced. The boys were ordered to the school room. The pieces of Richard's exercise book were examined. A dozen boys had seen its owner standing neat the shed before the fire originated. The teachers were sent to examine the closets for further evidence. Not only were several cards of matches found in Richard's closet, but also part of the printed envelope that had enclosed them. This piece of paper was a portion of the wrapper, of which the other part had been found in the shed.

These facts were duly announced to the boys, and it seemed as clear as noonday that Richard Grant was the incendiary. He was ordered to report forthwith at the office, and the boys were dismissed for the night.

"We have fixed him this time," said Nevers, in a whisper, as he and Redman left the room.

"He is under arrest, and to-morrow he will be sent home in disgrace," replied Redman, rubbing his hands. "Nevers, you will be the next captain of Company D."

"We have broken the fellows' idol, at any rate. Grant will spend the night in the guard house," added Nevers.

Nevers was slightly mistaken; for Richard, though he did not appear in Barrack B that night, occupied the guest chamber of Colonel Brockridge's private residence. His friends, especially Bailey, were gloomy and sad. The more lukewarm ones were sure, and always had been, that Grant was a bad boy.

On Monday morning, when the boys had assembled in the school room, Colonel Brockridge appeared, followed by Richard. The students understood that the incendiary case was to be settled, and a breathless silence pervaded the hall.

"Grant stands before you accused of a very grave offence," the principal began. "We cannot permit a boy who sets fire to a building to remain in the Institute. If guilty, he must be expelled. But Grant assures me this is a conspiracy to injure him. He declares that there is a secret organiza-

tion in the Institute called the Regulators, who
have determined to drive him away from the school
Some of us have heard of such an institution before, but its existence has never been clearly proved.
Redman, do you know any thing of such an association."

"I never heard of it before, sir," replied Redman.

"Do you, Nevers?"

"No, sir."

"Grant charges you both with being connected
with the Regulators."

"Let him prove it," said Nevers, in defiant
tones.

"Who is Dobbin?" asked the principal.

"I never heard the name before," answered Nevers. "I think it is very hard to be accused without evidence. I hope you will make Grant prove
what he says, sir."

"I will, my chief," said Richard, at a nod from
the colonel; and, without giving the source of his
information, he told all he knew about the Regulators.

"How many officers have the Regulators?" asked

Mr. Gault, rising from his chair, at the farther end of the room.

" *One, whom all obey*," replied Richard, repeating what he had heard on the island.

" Who is he ? "

" *Nevers.*"

" Are there traitors among us ? " continued Mr. Gault.

" *Not a traitor.*"

" What shall be done to him who discloses the secrets of the Regulators ? " asked the teacher.

" *He shall be pounded till he is black and blue, and, as man and boy, be despised till the end of his life*," replied Richard, repeating the words of the Regulators as nearly as he could remember them.

" What do you think of this, Nevers ? " asked the colonel.

" I don't know what it all means, sir," answered he, with a well-counterfeited look of astonishment.

There were a great many pale faces, beating hearts, and quivering lips in the seats, for it was certain that the daylight had been shining in upon the dark doings of the Regulators. Who was the traitor? who had betrayed the secrets of the fraternity? Confusion and trembling overwhelmed the Regulators.

" Before we proceed any farther," continued the principal, " if there are any of this secret band present who wish to acknowledge their guilt, and are willing to be forgiven, they may stand."

The silence was intense and deep. Nevers and Redman did not move a muscle, but some of the mutineers glanced at each other, and seemed to be in doubt.

" Now is the only time for confession," added the colonel.

Half a dozen boys rose; then one after another followed their example, till it seemed as if the whole band intended to absolve themselves from their vows. Those who rose were ordered to the rear of the room. Only ten of the band decided to abide the issue. They were called out by name.

" Here are the rest of the Regulators," said the colonel, when the obdurate ones had taken their places upon the platform.

Mr. Gault told his story, and Richard told his. The evidence was complete and overwhelming. Two of the teachers had been concealed in the shed, and had seen Redman set it on fire, and scatter the pieces of the exercise book in the vicinity. Another had seen Masters place the matches in Richard's closet. The colonel, knowing the details of the plot beforehand, had arranged every thing so as to insure the conviction of the conspirators.

" Boys," said Colonel Brockridge, " I am happy to inform you that Grant is entirely innocent."

Those in their seats received this announcement with a storm of applause.

" I knew he was innocent from the beginning."

Another burst of applause.

The principal detailed with great minuteness particulars of the conspiracy, with which our readers are already familiar. The ten Regulators were expelled at once, and sent away by the next train that left Tunbrook. The whole forenoon was occupied in disposing of the matter; but when the boys were sent out, there was no end to the cheering for Richard Grant.

It was plain that Nevers and Redman were the head and front of the Regulators. They were the authors of the association, and when they had gone, the organization died a natural death. Leslie was Kennedy, as Nevers was Dobbin. All the secrets and signs were bandied about and laughed at among the boys. Those of the band who remained were punished by being deprived of various privileges; but they behaved themselves afterwards with commendable propriety. One of them ventured to say "watermelons," one day, when he was angry with Richard, but a hundred boys hissed him for it.

Three of the expelled Regulators were eventually restored, but the lesson they had learned was all-sufficient.

Richard's victory was complete; and the events we have related rendered him a greater favorite than before. At the spring election he was chosen captain of Company D, and was regarded as the best officer in the line.

Richard's victory over himself was as complete

as that over the Regulators. That good resolution, kept through trial and temptation, eventually reformed his life and character. During the spring vacation, he spent a week at home, and rejoiced the hearts of Bertha and his father by the evidences of his reformation. Ben wept for joy, and Noddy Newman "couldn't tell, for the life of him, what had come over Dick."

Richard continued two years longer at Tunbrook, and maintained the high character he had won to the last. He was a favorite with the boys, and with the teachers. Colonel Brockridge pointed with pride to Major Grant — which was the title of our hero during the last year of his residence at Tunbrook — as one of the brightest ornaments of his school, and as one of the best fruits of his system of education.

And now we must take leave of Richard Grant; and we do so with greater regret than we should have done when his reputation was stained by "watermelons" and "sleep-walking."

Our hero is still true to himself. As we use fictitious names, our sympathizing readers will not be able to recognize Colonel Richard Grant, commanding a brigade in the Army of the Potomac, at the present time; but, true to his country in her hour of peril, he has served with that gallant band of brave men from the commencement of the war.

If my young friends would conquer others; if they would be chosen of men to reign in the hearts of their fellow-beings, and thus guide the destinies of men and nations; if they would be chosen of God to do his work in earth and heaven, — they must first conquer themselves.